MW00953907

Ghost Writer

BY RICK JUST

Also by Rick Just

Fiction
Keeping Private Idaho
Wizard Chase
Wizard Girl
Wizards' End
Anjel

Non-Fiction
Idaho Snapshots

In Memory of Mary Kelly McColl

Prologue

Sticky wire held her legs and arms and hair. She pulled away with a sound like Velcro ripping, but that made the wire stick somewhere else. Not wire, really. Too thin for that. She struggled against it, getting more caught up in the stuff with every move. She stopped to catch her breath. Yet, she still moved. Vibrated. Something plucked the strands, testing them as if tuning an elaborate guitar. From the edge of her vision she saw a black sickle flick a silent note. She felt it vibrate with bass in her bones. Not wire. Web!

She jolted awake, sweating, heart racing, gasping for breath. For a moment, she dared not move in case her arms and legs were really wrapped in a tight cocoon.

With great effort she rolled her head to one side, testing her tethers. No sticky strands pinning her to the bed. So. Just a dream. Just her worst nightmare, ever. The digital clock next to her bed read 12:01. She was now officially fourteen. She did not feel like celebrating.

JUNE 2014

Sunday	Monday	Tuesday	Wednesday	Thursday	Friday	Saturday
1	2	3	4	5	6	7
8	9	10	11	12	13	14
15 B Day!	16	17	18	19	20	21
22	23	24	25	26	27	28
29	30					

For a few more seconds, Sam held the future in her hands. Stretching out the suspense a little, she hefted gift. A little heavy, maybe. It was wider than what she was hoping for, and maybe a bit thinner. She wasn't certain how they were packaged. This felt more like an iPad than an iPhone. Only one way to find out.

Tearing off the wrapping, she folded back the tissue paper to reveal a leather cover. For a second, she thought the present was at least something she might like. She had not asked for an iPad or a Kindle. She could get excited about either. Leather cover. She had never seen a tablet with a cover that said diary on the front. Still...

Sam lifted the cover with her fingers, thinking there was a teeny tiny chance a welcome screen would appear beneath it. Nope. Pages. Dozens and dozens of desolate blank pages.

"I know you were hoping for a phone," her dad said.

"Maybe we can swing that for Christmas. This is pretty cool, though, right?"

He was so needy. Sam did her best to muster some enthusiasm for the gift.

"Sure, cool. Thanks."

Her dad said, "Hey, they do a lot of the same things, you know. You can write on this, you can carry it around in your purse." He paused for a minute, gears going, trying to think of the possibly several ways in which a diary was like an iPhone. "You can draw in it. You can make lists..."

When Sam's frown did not turn upside down, he said, "Hey, kiddo, this really is a neat thing. It's an antique, maybe a hundred years old. That's real leather and I bet that's real gold embossing."

"Embossing?"

"Yeah, the lettering on the cover."

The lettering, gold, embossed, whatever, said "DIARY." Big whoop.

"It's like an heirloom," he went on. "I found it at the Big House. It was hidden behind a dresser in the wall."

"In the wall? How do you hide something in a wall?"

"That was the cool part. Someone had gone to a lot of trouble to hide it. There was a board that fit an opening about a foot square. The board was covered with wallpaper, just like the rest of the wall, and the pattern matched with the paper on the wall perfectly. There was a tiny little finishing nail in the board. You could barely see it, but if you pulled on it with your fingers, the whole thing came out and—voila—there's the diary hidden behind it."

Sam flipped through a couple pages.

"Why would anyone hide an empty diary?"

Her dad shrugged. "I don't know. Maybe they were saving it there all this time just for you. That's what I thought, anyway, when I found it."

Sam's dad spent all his spare time working on the "Big House." His great-grandparents built it in the 1800s. No one had lived there since Sam's great aunt died in 1990. Sam's dad was going through all the old stuff and fixing it up. At least he said he was fixing it up. Sam could never see much progress. She didn't know why he was doing it in the first place. He wasn't planning to rent it out or anything, as far as she knew. He was restoring it, the way it had been 150 or so years ago. Like anyone would ever care.

The Big House wasn't even big. He called it that because his great grandparents had called it that. Maybe it was big compared to the log cabin they had lived in before.

It was barely a house, all run down with broken windows that let birds come and go whenever they liked. Okay, he *had* fixed the windows, and he had cleaned up the bird poop. But there was so much else to do before anyone could live in it. None of the sinks or toilets worked. There wasn't even electricity in the house. The roof leaked. And, it smelled. It smelled like mice and crumbling paper and old people.

The house smelled warm, but it was always cold. It could be 105 outside and inside the house it felt like maybe 60. Her dad actually bragged about that. He went on and on about how thick the brick walls were—"seven bricks thick." Which was fine, in the summer, but what about winter? Had he thought about how cold it would get then? That was another thing. It didn't have a furnace. It had this stove the size of a Miata in the kitchen. They had cooked everything on that and had used it for heat, too. That meant someone had to chop wood all the time. There was a big box next to the stove where they piled the wood. Now, it was just full of spiders. The thought of that made Sam shudder.

"And, mostly, you can use it to capture all your thoughts," he said.

Yeah, right. Sam had some thoughts she could capture.

"Throw me a pen," she said, to no one in particular.

Her mom, who at least had the good sense not to add any features to her dad's list of ways a diary was like an iPhone, pulled a ballpoint from the cup on the counter and tossed it to her.

Sam opened up the diary a few pages in and started to write.

"Shouldn't you start at the beginning?" her dad asked.

She glared at him.

"Okay, okay. Do it any way you want."

Oh, that's exactly what she had in mind

Dear diary: Today is my birthday, June 15, 2014. I am 14 years old. I asked for an iPhone for my birthday so I could quit using this crappy old hand me down piece of junk I carry around now. Guess what?!?! I got this crappy diary instead!

She closed the pen between the pages and gave the diary a pat.

"What did you write?" her dad asked.

"Chris! You can't ask her that," her mom said. "A diary is private."

He put his hands up as if fending off seagulls. "Right, right. My bad. It's your business. That's what it's for." He narrowed his eyes. "Where ya gonna hide it?"

***

Hailey's texted reply was predictable: *WTF!?!*

WTF stood for What The Fudge. Anyway, that's what Hailey told her Mormon parents, who were super conservative. Sam thought Hailey was switched at birth. She was probably the daughter of gypsies or members of a biker gang. She even looked gypsy-like, with short, dark hair. Everyone else in her family had blond hair.

Sam texted back, *Really. I think I'm sposd to wear pigtails now.*

Sounds like something my units wd do.

Hailey called her parents "units" or "parental units," unless she was totally exasperated with them, at which time they became the "aliens."

Before Sam could respond, Hailey texted, *Hey, ht gy alrt. Lifeguard at the pool. I wd so hit that!*

Sam liked guys, at least sometimes. Hailey obsessed about them. Next she would be...

Savior substance, give it, give it!

And, there it was. In Hailey's world, "savior substance" was makeup. If she obsessed about boys, she obsessed about makeup even more. Her parents wouldn't let her come within a block of the stuff, so she counted on Sam to keep her supplied. Sam could sneak a little once in a while from her mom. Never enough to satisfy the makeup hound.

I can't get more rt nw. She's running low.

Dam. May b borrow sum.

No! Dont! I see what can do.

"Borrow" was Hailey's word for shoplift. She was good at it. Not so good she could get away with it forever. When they'd go into a store together, Sam noticed the clerks watched them like they'd just been released from a super max prison. It made her feel creepy. She was sure someone would catch Hailey any day, now. Because they were always together, that meant she'd be in trouble, too.

Sam didn't steal stuff. Well, not much. She'd kiped her share of candy as a kid. And, last winter, she'd stolen a scarf for her mother for Christmas. That gave Sam the guilts every time her mother wore it.

Just nd a ltl blush. & eyeliner.

ok. Blush maybe.

cool. Ltr.

Time to dig out the empty Curiously Strong Mints can. Hailey had a matching one with her, apparently empty. The routine was that Sam would sneak into the master bath when her mom was outside and scrape a little face dust into the mint can from her dresser drawer. Next time she saw Hailey, they'd swap cans.

This conspiracy of makeup had started about two years earlier. Sam couldn't steal much from her mother because her mom hardly used any makeup. Hailey joked that her mom had the same tube of lipstick she'd used when she got married.

Sam's mom wasn't exactly a cosmetics queen, but she did use a little of everything. Taking a tiny amount was easy enough for blush and eyeliner. Lip gloss and mascara were another matter. You kind of needed the whole thing.

Rachel, Sam's older sister, was a bonanza for makeup miners. When she came home from college Sam could usually sneak a bottle of lip gloss or a mascara brush from her without her noticing. Their mom was so neat with everything Sam felt almost like she had to measure the distance between the containers to make sure they were exactly, precisely, absolutely in the right spot when she put them back. Rachel's makeup table looked like the products were placed by grenade, with multiples of everything. Sam thought she could probably sweep about a fourth of it off the table and into a box without her sister even noticing.

Unfortunately, her mom couldn't possibly keep the makeup junkie supplied, and Rachel wouldn't be home for a few more days. Hailey wore it thick and often. She was always having to wash it all off for five minutes because one of her siblings might see her. Her older sister, Hannah, was a senior who shared their mother's disdain for cosmetics. Hailey could usually avoid her between classes, but she would have to strip it all off to go to lunch, then reapply. Then she'd wash it off again so Hannah or her little brothers wouldn't catch her wearing it on the bus. Any one of them would turn her in to the parental units if they saw a stray smear of eye shadow.

When her parents caught her—and they caught her

often—the makeup went out with the banana peels and used dental floss.

Mormons weren't all anti-makeup fanatics. Sam knew plenty of Mormon girls in school who would make Rachel look like an amateur when it came to makeup. The makeup aversion was something in Hailey's mother's genes.

Why keeping Hailey supplied with makeup was her problem, Sam couldn't really say. They were BFFs. And BFFs didn't let each other go to jail.

It was the sort of thing one might put in a diary. If one were inclined to ever open the crappy thing again.

***

Sam's mom had tried to get her interested in having a birthday party. Like, really? She was fourteen, not four. Besides, who would she invite? Oh, there were some girls she could think of. Maybe even a couple of boys. Again, if she were four. Maybe three our four boys, if… If she was going to have a party, which she was totally NOT.

In the first place, why would she inflict her parents on kids she knew from school? Her parents weren't awful, or anything, just lame. Normally lame, she supposed. It was lame acknowledging that you had parents at all.

And those girls—and certainly those boys—were not really her friends. They were just kids she knew at school. Hailey was her friend. Her BFF. She didn't need anyone else. She could invite Hailey, but Hailey was over all the time. Way more than Sam was at Hailey's place, because parents.

No one had weirder parents that Hailey. Yeah,

Mormon, but Momon to the max! They didn't drink—even coffee or coke—or smoke. Yes, water and milk, but no tea. Maybe they drank Nehi, Sam wasn't sure. They never, ever swore. Okay, she'd heard Mrs. Poulsen say "fudge" once. That was shocking. Usually, she just said "word," or "good word."

The wierdest thing about them was what Sam's mom was talking about right now over birthday cake, shared by just the three of them after supper.

"So, how is everyone over at the Poulsen's?" her mom asked. It sounded like an innocent question. Sam knew it was really a little dig. One her mom could never resist.

"Everyone's fine, Mom. No one has the plague or anything."

The Poulsens didn't believe in vaccines. They were afraid it would make their kids autistic, or something. It rankled Sam's mom.

"Give it a rest, hon," her dad said.

"Give what a rest? I simply asked…"

"I know, I know. You just asked how they are. Just let it be."

Sam's mom bunched up her brow. "I didn't mean a thing by it. I'm concerned, that's all. About Hailey, mostly."

Sam rolled her eyes. "She's fine, Mom."

And her mom dropped the subject. For a minute.

At a minute and one second she said, "It just bothers me that they think its okay to endanger everyone else in the community, that's all."

"Oh, for Pete's sake, Amanda," her dad said. "No one

else is getting hurt because they don't vaccinate their kids." He gave his wife a hard look. "No one got smallpox because I didn't get a shot."

As soon as he said it, her dad gave Sam a sideways glance as if he regretted it. The look just begged her to ask.

"What about smallpox? You didn't get a shot?" she asked. "Weren't you supposed to."

"Well…"

"Dad?"

"Not exactly," he said.

"Put your foot in it, didn't you?" Her mom said.

Sam said, "What's 'not exactly'?"

"Well, when I was in fourth grade… Maybe it was fifth grade. Somewhere along in there. Anyway, we were getting smallpox shots. I hated shots. I mean, I really, really hated them. I'd had what seemed like a million of them by then, polio, diptheria…"

"Polio isn't a shot," Sam said. "It's oral."

"Yeah, I know. The first ones weren't though. They were shots."

"You got a polio shot?" her mom asked. "I just took sugar pills." Then she added, "Of course, you're much, much older than I am."

Sam expected her mom to call him a cradle robber. She'd heard that a million times. Her dad was 12 years older than her mom.

"Yeah, I took cubes or something, too. But I think I got a shot once," he said. "Anyway, I got shots. Whatever they were for. I was tired of it. So for smallpox, we had to stand in a really long line to get them and there was this kid about a dozen kids in front of me that pitched a fit. I mean, he stomped up and down like he was running in place and just shrieked at the top of his lungs when they gave him his shot."

"Baby," his wife said.

"Whatever. It scared me. So, while everyone was staring it this kid and listening to him holler, I just ducked out of line. They'd already marked me off as being present and no one noticed."

"Baby," Amanda said, again, this time pointedly at her husband.

He stuck his tongue out at her.

"Funny thing was," he went on, "My mom wanted to see my shot when I got home."

"Really? What was there to see," Sam said.

"I know, right? But smallpox wasn't like most vaccinations. They just scratch your arm to get it into your system. So, I told her I had to go to the bathroom first. While I was in there I got a needle and scratched my bicep."

"And she bought that?" Sam asked.

"Well, yeah. She didn't know what it looked like, exactly."

"And now your big, brave dad is proud because he doesn't have a smallpox vaccine scar like just about everyone else who's as ancient as he is," Sam's mom said.

"So, there was still smallpox when you were a kid?" Sam asked.

Her mom said, "Sure. And dinosaurs. Which brings

me back to the point. They wiped out smallpox because everyone got a shot. They wiped out polio the same way."

"Not quite," Chris said.

"Right, not quite," Amanda went on. "There are still a few cases that show up in Africa. India, too, I think. But it's nearly wiped out. It would be if people like the Poulsens would just get their shots."

That didn't make sense to Sam. "But they're not going to Africa. They don't need polio shots."

"Maybe not polio. They don't get shots for anything, though," her mother said. "And nothing stops people from Africa from coming here. They could still get polio. Or measles. Measles was wiped out in the U.S. until someone brought it into New York City where people who hadn't been vaccinated caught it."

"I had measles," Chris said, almost in a whisper.

"And you didn't die," said Amanda. "Lucky you! But you don't need luck anymore, just a vaccination."

JUNE 2014

Sunday	Monday	Tuesday	Wednesday	Thursday	Friday	Saturday
1	2	3	4	5	6	7
8	9	10	11	12	13	14
15 B Day!	16	17	18	19	20	21
22	23	24	25	26	27	28
29	30					

Sam spent the night tossing and turning with Hailey's makeup issue swirling around in her head. One minute she resolved to tell her to knock it off with the makeup. Hailey was pretty. She really didn't need any help. The next minute she realized the futility of that conversation. Hailey turned heads—boy heads—when she wore makeup.

Maybe Hailey could order it off the internet and have it sent to a friend. No, that would take money. Specifically, it would take a credit card. Another idea dead in the dust.

The internet. There was free stuff on the internet. DIY stuff.

At 3:30 in the morning, Sam slipped out of bed. She woke up her computer, squinting at the blinding glare from the screen. When her eyes adjusted, she tapped YOU into the URL window and the helpful search engine suggested that she might mean YouTube. She clicked on that, then typed "homemade makeup" into the YouTube search box.

Bam! There was a video about making your own makeup.

Slipping on earbuds, Sam watched for a little over seven minutes, learning that you could burn almonds—almonds!—to make a basic black powder, which they called coal. You could mix the coal with honey and use an empty applicator to make mascara. To make eyeliner, you just mixed it with olive oil. So easy!

Sam wanted to make some notes. She felt around on her desk for a pencil. They were all hiding. She looked around and spotted the crappy diary on the nightstand. The pen she used earlier was still in it.

Sam scooted her chair back by kicking up her legs, sending her across the room in a practiced move. She half-turned and flipped the diary open to retrieve the pen. She had already shut it when something made her stop. Her eye had registered a lot more writing than she thought she had done.

Sam lifted the leather cover of the diary and saw that the first page was full of writing. Someone's writing. Not hers.

Oh my god, she thought. Not just a crappy old diary, but a crappy used diary. She wondered why she hadn't noticed that before. The writing was neat. It was—and she didn't remember when she last used this word—elegant.

Sam flipped the page back and saw two more entries, dated June 13 and June 14, 1914. Glancing through it she didn't see much that interested her. Then she turned the page again and found her own entry, dated yesterday, June 15, 2014. The first thought she had was how awful her handwriting was, compared with the earlier entries.

Sam did a double take. There was another entry after hers. It was dated June 15, 1914.

What is this writing? Someone is playing a trick on me! I really must find a better hiding place.

That was it. Sam read it again. Then she read her entry, and read the entry after it, again. Then she read every entry.

June 12, 1914

My first entry. Father gave me this lovely diary for my 14th birthday. With it I can practice my penmanship & record the days of my life.

What to write? The weather is nice. Maybe I should be more specific. It is a most pleasant day with very few clouds. The sky is the color of a robin's egg. Lighter than some days. I hear that means we may have a hot afternoon. That is something I can report in tomorrow's entry.

But what to write, really? This is just for me so just my thoughts will do. Do I have thoughts? Yes, of course, but any worth writing down? Maybe I should simply write down what I do during the day. I do not lead an adventurous life. I would risk boring my reader, who is me! Which is me?

Or, will someone else read this one day? Certainly not soon, I hope. If I have thoughts worthy of the pen, I want to keep them to myself for now. But someday, maybe, someone might read this, long after I die. I must keep that in mind. Maybe there are thoughts that are too private.

Too private for someone to read fifty or one hundred years hence? I will not be here to care, I suppose. So, hello, future. I hope you are having a good day.

It was a joke. Darn him! Her father must have set this up. Sam imagined him sneaking into her room—when? It would have taken a few minutes to write all that down. She tried to think of when he could have done it. They'd had dinner together, birthday cake, talked about vaccinations, watched TV, then gone to bed. She couldn't think of when he might have written this.

June 13, 1914

Cool. Not hot as the color of the sky portended.

Last night Sidney and Madeline went to the Roxy to see "Tess of the Storm Country." They thot it was fine & so did Mary and Maggie. They went to see it Monday night & stayed to see it thru twice. Mary is going to get the book from a friend of hers.

I have been reading "Eben Holder" by Bacheller this morning. Also, embroidering on my night gown.

Miss Wetzel came over this afternoon & we sewed until supper was ready. After supper Miss Wetzel played & Mary & Mamma & the boys sang. After we once get things started here she never gets to go home until late, but then, we all have a good time.

Strawberries beginning to ripen.

That so did not sound like her dad. What did he know about books and movies from 1914? Or, did he know? He was a nut for history.

June 13, 1914

Rain and rain. Isn't this supposed to be summer?

Started today putting a solution of Borax and water on my head to cure the dandruff.

The old hen stepped on one of the little ducks today and broke its leg, so we will have to keep it in the house for a while.

Oh, and I went down to Bithell's. Laura taught me how to make the dearest little basket out of pine needles.

We had fresh corn and tomatoes for supper & I love them both, but that was the first time I'd had any this year. Also had fried chicken for breakfast—the first time this summer.

And is it summer? Again, it is raining!!!!!!!

It didn't look like his handwriting. His wasn't any better than her own. This was beautiful. Maybe her mother.

Whoever it was could have written most of this before she ever tore the wrapping off. She hadn't looked at every page. Then, they could have crept into her room and scribbled down the little entry after what she had written.

But it was not scribbled. It was carefully written.

So, she would lay a trap. Not much of one, but a trap, still.

Early, early morning, June 16, 2014

Cute. Real cute, Dad. Is this supposed to make me want to write in this diary? This <u>crappy</u> used diary!!! Well, it's not going to work. You can consider this the last time I am ever going to write a word!

***

Sam wanted to kill her mother the third time she yelled "Breakfast!" up the stairs. Instead, she screamed into her pillow, then raised her head and yelled, "Coming!"

She rolled out of bed and stared at the clock for a moment, trying to make sense of the numbers: 9:07. Her dad would already have gone to work. That was okay. They didn't often eat breakfast together in the summer. She wasn't in the mood to share breakfast with him, anyway. He was such a dork for that diary trick.

Speaking of the diary, she grabbed it and threw it under her mattress. Then, thinking better of it, she dug it out and looked at her last entry. It was the last entry, so her dad hadn't snuck in and messed with it while she was sleeping. Good. Back under the mattress it went.

"I thought I was going to have to call in the National Guard to get you out of bed."

"Mumph."

"Good morning to you, too."

"Morning."

"How does it feel to be 14?"

"Duh, like 13, only a day older."

Her mother slid a spatula full of scrambled eggs and a slice of bacon right out of the fry pan onto her plate.

"I think Dad was a little disappointed by your reaction to the present he got you."

Sam gave her mother a stare.

"What? He put a lot of thought into it."

"Mom, he *found* it. He found it and then he wrapped it up and gave it to me."

"Well, you could still have shown a little more appreciation. That diary means a lot to him."

"To him? Well, why didn't he just keep it, then?"

Her mom sat down across the table from her, a kitchen towel still clutched in one hand.

"Sam, he wanted to share it with you. That's what

makes it a special gift. He gave you something he really treasures."

"That sucks."

"Sam."

"I mean, really, Mom, why couldn't he give me something I'd treasure. Like a new iPhone!"

"Honey, you'll get an iPhone. It's just that things are really, really tight right now with the Big House needing so much."

"Like I don't need an iPhone, but that house needs floorboards, right?"

"Well, it does. And it needs..."

"It needs a new house, is what it needs. Dad should tear it down and sell the land. Then things wouldn't be 'really, really tight.'"

Her mother was quiet for a moment. When she spoke it was with a measured calm that Sam recognized as her serious voice.

"Dad's great-grandparents built the Big House. It's not just a house to him. It's his history. Honey, it's your history, too."

"I'd rather have an iPhone than history."

Her mother rolled her eyes, and said, "If we got you an iPhone, you'd want another one in a year. A new one. There's always a better one coming out. You can never keep up. History is forever. It doesn't change."

Sam took a bite of eggs. She hadn't quite finished chewing them when she said, "Yeah, it'll always be there. Meanwhile, I have to text on practically a crank telephone."

***

So, blush, blush, blush!??

Sam texted back, *Yes yes ys. And more.*

What more?

Eyliner and mascara.

Joking?! 4 real?

Real real. Learned how make it.

Hailey had the fastest thumbs in the West. When she didn't text back instantly, Sam thought she'd had a stroke.

Jok?

No joke. Youtuve.

What?

YouTube. Bring almonds.

Seriously??

Almonds. If youhave any, bring them. I have honey.

***

Hailey lived about a mile away. Sam would swear it wasn't two minutes before Hailey skidded her bike into the driveway and ran up the concrete steps.

"Almonds?" she said, when Sam opened the side door.

"Shh!"

In a low voice Hailey asked, "Almonds are a secret?"

"Makeup is a secret. Like always. C'mon."

They pounded up the stairs to Sam's room and closed the door behind them. Hailey dug in her backpack and pulled out a quart Ziploc full of nuts.

"These have sugar on them."

"So? Does that make a difference?"

Sam shrugged. "We'll see. Oh, crap. I forgot to get the

other stuff from the kitchen."

The two of them ran into the hall and launched themselves down the stairs, hitting about one out of three with their heels.

"Girls! Can you walk like humans, please?"

"Sorry," said Sam.

"Sorry, Mrs. Reed," said Hailey.

When they got to the kitchen, Sam handed Hailey a bear-shaped bottle of honey she'd snagged off the counter, then started opening cabinet doors. On the third try she found the olive oil. They turned and raced toward the stairs.

"Walk-ing," said Mrs. Reed from the dining room.

They quickly tip-toed up the stairs and into Sam's bedroom where, again, they closed the door, laughing.

"Now what?" Hailey whispered.

"Now we cook this up in the Library."

The Library was once the Club House, the Little House, and the Treehouse. The moniker had changed over the years; the place had changed little. As the girls grew up, they adapted its use to their changing needs. Yes, it once had a sign that said "No Boys Allowed." That was soooo long ago. When they were little, they served tea to toys in the Little House. They held totally secret meetings there with girlfriends. Now, as the Library, it was where they kept a few books and magazines they didn't want their parents to know about.

Once, there was a good, solid ladder that made it easy for little girls to climb to the structure in the tree. Sam's dad had made both the tree house and the ladder.

Carpentry was a hobby of his, so this little project—begun when Sam was three and Rachel was nine—was more elaborate than your average tree house. It had a small deck where two or three girls could sit in folding chairs or dangle their legs over the edge and watch the sunset. Inside there was a pretend kitchen, a table with four kid-sized chairs, and a two-person sleeping loft that you had to climb up to on a ladder.

Rachel had owned the tree house for the first three years of its life. When she outgrew it, Sam took over. Sam and Hailey, really. They couldn't remember when they had not been best friends.

A couple of years ago, the ladder got rickety, so Sam's dad, took it down for repairs. He was busy working on the Big House, even back then. At first, Sam nagged him about fixing the ladder. That was before she and Hailey discovered a way to get into the tree and the tree house without it. Two ways, really. From the ground, you could get a little run going up the leaning trunk of the big willow and just before you were about to fall over backward, you could grab a handy limb, then another, and pull yourself up. That made the tree house even more their exclusive territory than it was before, since no one else knew the secret. Even better, they soon figured out that one of the big limbs had grown close enough to Sam's bedroom window that they only risked their lives a little every time they jumped from the sill to the limb or vice versa.

The Library had a hotplate Sam and Hailey had long ago used for making cocoa and heating up soup. They wouldn't need to run the extension cord for that into her room today, but the battered saucepan collecting dust on top of it would come in handy.

Sam dumped a few of the almonds into the pan. Then she looked at them for a minute.

"What?" Hailey asked.

"We need to burn them. It's burnt almonds that make the black stuff."

"Okay. So how do you do that?"

"I don't know," Sam said. "That's what I was trying to figure out."

"Hotplate?"

"I think they really need to be on fire. Like, you have to hold them over a match or something."

"We've got matches. Wait, even better, we've got candles."

Hailey looked through one of the tiny drawers in the pretend kitchen and found a half-used book of matches. She struck one and held it to the blackened wick of a votive candle they used for light during summer sleepovers. "There ya go," she said.

Sam gave her a suspicious look.

"Hey, I lit the candle and brought the almonds," Hailey said.

"Yeah, but you're the one who wants the makeup. I'm not going to burn my fingers."

Hailey plucked an almond out of the plastic bag. Holding the very tip with her carefully-pointed fingernails, she moved the nut over the flame. "Chicken," she muttered, as she did it.

The sugar coating on the almond began to crackle and bubble. A little tendril of smoke climbed up from the surface. A second later, Hailey dropped the nut.

"Shit!"

Hailey sucked on her fingers while Sam found the blackened almond on the floor.

"It works," Sam said. "Anyway, it works a little. We need to make a whole lot more of it."

"Nu-uh, not with my fingers."

"Do you want mascara?"

"I *need* mascara. But I need my fingers, too."

That was hard to argue with. Sam thought about it for a moment.

"I bet we could do it with the barbecue lighter. You know, that long-necked gizmo Dad uses to fire up the grill."

"What good would that do? We've got flame, we need a way to hold the nuts without burning my fingers."

"We put them in the pan and move the end of the lighter over them while they burn."

"Might work."

"I'll go get it."

Sam left the Library, dropped down onto the limb near her bedroom, and stepped through her window, ducking so she wouldn't bang her head. She was nearly out the door when something occurred to her. She reached under her mattress and felt for the diary.

"Hey," she called up to Hailey.

Hailey's head appeared over the edge of the deck.

"Take a look at this while I'm gone. Tell me what you think."

Hailey dropped down on the limb beneath the deck and reached for the leather bound volume.

***

It took Sam a little more time than she'd expected to get the lighter. She knew right where it was, but she realized they might need to crush the almonds while burning them. She rattled around looking for something on her dad's workbench in the garage for a few minutes, finally settling on a big rusty bolt with a round head. It looked like it was scrap, so her dad probably wouldn't mind if she messed it up. She also picked up the oldest, worst looking hammer she could find, under the theory that he wouldn't miss it much if she forgot to bring it back, which was her tendency, especially if she got distracted by something.

When she got back to the Library, Hailey was sitting on the floor, legs crossed, concentrating on the diary.

"What do you think?"

Hailey looked up. "What *is* this?" she asked. "Is your dad messing with you?"

"Probably. It's just the sort of lame joke he'd pull."

"Yeah, I suppose. Really excellent handwriting, though."

"I know. Isn't that weird? I've never seen him write like that before." Sam thought for a moment. "I don't think I've ever seen anyone write that good."

"Maybe a teacher," Hailey said.

"Maybe my mom. Her writing's better than Dad's. I

don't think she can write like that, though."

"What does it mean Palmer Method?"

"Palmer Method? What are you talking about?"

Hailey turned the diary around and pointed. "Right here."

There, right below her last entry was this:

June 16, 1914

Is this the work of the devil? Or does someone mean me to think that? I think someone is having a trick on me! The writing is terrible enough that it might have come from the hand of my little brother. It seems the writing of an eight-year-old or someone who has not studied the Palmer Method.

This would suggest I need to find a better hiding place. I have just the place in mind and the method of hiding it as well.

Sam sat staring at the diary long enough for Hailey to say, "Earth to Sam. Do you read me, Sam?" She snapped her fingers in front of Sam's face.

Sam looked up, narrowing her eyes. "Did you write this?"

"Me? How would I write it? You handed it to me a few minutes ago."

"This last part, did you write that?"

"The last entry?"

Sam nodded.

"No. I didn't write any of it. But you wrote some of it, right? The part about the crappy diary? That sounds like you."

"Of course, I wrote that. You swear you didn't write

that last part? Pinky swear?"

"Pinky swear? What are you, nine?"

"Okay, then swear that you'll never use makeup again, if you're lying."

"What's got into you?"

"Swear!"

"Yes, yes. I swear I won't ever use makeup again, if I'm lying. Which is no big deal, because I. Am. Not!"

Sam's hands felt like they could barely hold up the diary. What was going on?

"I looked at this, like, maybe an hour ago. That last entry wasn't there."

"The Palmer Method thing?"

"Yeah. That was the first time I read that. Dad's not here, so he couldn't have done it. Mom's here, but she hasn't even been upstairs all morning."

"What are you saying?"

"Someone wrote it!"

"Well, yeah. As a joke, right?"

"No kidding! But who was it?"

"Where did you have it?"

"Under my mattress."

"Not the most original hiding place."

"I know, but so what? No one was up here but you and me all morning. If you didn't write it, who did?"

"I swear, jumping up and down on my mother's grave, I didn't write it!" said Hailey. "I don't even have a pen."

Sam looked back down at the writing and noticed

something else about it.

"Look at this. It's like a fountain pen or calligraphy or something."

There was a smoothness to the writing that was unlike anything the girls were used to seeing. It was almost as if someone had painted the letters, joining them together in sweeping loops and forming extravagant curls.

"Look at my writing," Sam said.

"Sucks," said Hailey.

"Bite me. Just look at the letters. All the lines are about the same. But look at the way the words are formed here. See how the lines of the letters are thin, then thick, then thin again. That's from a fountain pen, I think. Maybe even a quill pen."

"What's a quill pen?"

"Like a feather."

"Oh, yeah. They'd dip it in ink to write with."

They sat there looking at each other, letting their minds race. After a moment, Hailey broke the silence.

"Who writes with feathers?"

"Benjamin Franklin."

"Seriously?"

"The queen of England? I don't know. Really, really old people."

"You mean dead people."

"Dead people don't write."

As if their chins were on the same string, the girls looked down at the page with the beautiful writing. And the Sam writing.

"This is nuts," Sam said.

Hailey snorted. "Almonds, actually." She picked up one and popped it in her mouth.

"Someone has to be doing this!"

"Big duh. But, who?"

"Maybe Dad, somehow."

"How, somehow?"

"I don't know! Maybe it's not him. It's somebody who can sneak in and out of my room."

"Okay, so it pretty much has to be me, then."

Sam widened her eyes.

Hailey said, "I'm totally kidding! I don't write any better than you do."

"Mom, then."

"Or your dad, I guess." Hailey slapped the floor. "Wait!"

"What?"

"We can find out!"

"How?"

"Remember when my stupid little brother was coming into me and Hannah's room and messing with stuff?"

"Yeah, but... Oh, yeah! You caught him by using your webcam!"

"Right. I found this cool, like, spy video program for free. I caught him setting up all Hannah's stupid stuffed animals like they were having an orgy."

"So, we could set it up to see who writes in the diary."

"Yeah!"

"But I don't have a webcam."

"No worries. We'll use mine. It's not built in."

"And the software?"

"Like I said, free."

They abandoned the DIY makeup project, at least for the moment. Hailey got the software download started, then wheeled home to unplug her webcam. When they got it up and running, they placed the diary conspicuously on Sam's desk.

"Will this, like, fill up my whole hard drive?"

"Nah. We'll set it to record only when it senses movement," Hailey said. "Hey, are you gonna write something?"

"Like what?"

Hailey shrugged. "Whatever. It's your turn."

Sam thought about arguing that she wasn't taking turns. It did seem that way. She picked up a ballpoint and began to write.

June 16, about 11:30 am. Oh yeah, 2014

So, whoever is writing in this, just stop! You can't get away with it!

XOXOXO, Sam

Sam decided leaving the diary out wasn't enough. She opened it up, folded back the pages with the heel of her hand, and placed the pen on top of it, right below her latest entry. It was like baiting a mouse trap.

***

That evening, Sam kept a close eye on her parents and

on the stairs to her room. Their bedroom was up there too, down the hall from hers. She spotted her mother taking an armful of folded towels up the stairs and decided it was a great time to follow her.

Her mom headed for the hall linen closet. Sam stepped into her own room, turned on the light, and sat down on the bed. When her mother came back down the hall she went right on by, then stopped and poked her head in.

"Are you going to bed?"

Sam said, "Nah."

"Okay. I saw you sitting there staring off into space and wondered."

"Just thinking."

"Don't hurt yourself."

Sam stuck her tongue out at her mother. Her mother did the same, winked, and went back downstairs.

There was no chance—zero—that either of her parents had gone into her room. Sam almost left without checking the diary, but she couldn't resist.

She got up and went to the computer desk. There was another entry.

More lines had appeared since they set up the trap that morning. Sam picked up the pen. As she did, her finger brushed against the diary page, leaving a tiny smear of ink.

The ink was wet.

Without bothering to read the entry, Sam grabbed the mouse to wake up her computer. She navigated to the desktop window for the webcam recording. It was recording now, of course. She was moving around right in front of it.

She stopped the cam and scrolled it back. In choppy rewind she watched herself set the pen down, then saw her feet back away from the computer. She kept rewinding until she saw herself and Hailey messing around with the diary, backward, earlier in the day. She pressed stop, then play.

Between the time they had set the trap and the time she saw her feet walking into the range of the webcam, there was about two minutes of nothing.

Except, there was a little bump in the picture. She and Hailey went out of view and the recording blipped. At first, she couldn't say exactly what the change was. The light, maybe. It was morning when she and Hailey had been in front of the camera. When they left, the camera quit recording. Then it started again. You could tell because the light had changed. Had it started a few minutes ago when she switched on the light and entered the room? Maybe.

Sam moved the sound slider to the right and rewound the video. She started it again at the point where she and Hailey were leaving the room. Sam caught a little snatch of their conversation before the camera shut off. When the camera came on again, she could not hear anything. Well, maybe a little rustling. After about a minute she caught the short conversation she'd just had with her mom. The mic picked it up, but it was a little echoey. She watched her feet walk into view and saw her hands pick up the pen.

So, that was it. When she turned the light on, she triggered the camera. They had caught exactly no one.

Sam wound it back to when she turned on the light. This time she concentrated on the diary itself. The new entry was right there under her pen. How did someone sneak in and do that without starting the webcam?

Then, Sam saw something else. The entire new entry was not yet in place. But it was getting there. She watched as the words appeared, one letter at a time, snaking across the page and beneath the ballpoint pen. The writing continued, by itself until it reached the end of a sentence. It was when the neat little period appeared that Sam lost it.

"Oh shit! Oh shit! Oh shit!"

She kicked back in her chair propelling herself across the floor next to her bed. This trip lacked her earlier grace. The chair tipped and spilled her onto the carpet. She jumped up and onto her bed like rug sharks were after her.

Sam stood there in the center of her bed with her fists in her mouth. That muffled her continued, "Oh shit! Oh shit!"

"Honey?" her dad called up the stairs. "Are you okay?"

Was she okay? Well, if never having been so scared in her life was okay then, yeah, she was great.

"Y-yes. I just... I stubbed my toe on the chair."

"Did you break it?" This came from her mother.

"No, I'm fine. Hurts like heck, though."

"I bet. Try to find some better words to express your pain, okay sweetie?"

"Sorry, Mom."

As she had the raised voice conversation with her parents, Sam dug out her phone.

Oh Sht sht shit!!!!, she typed.

She pressed send and started to text a second message,

then realized this called for an actual conversation. She pressed connect.

"Shit what?" Hailey whispered into her phone.

"You're not going to believe it!"

"Tell me, tell me! Did you catch the mystery man? Was it your dad?"

"Yes. I mean, no. It wasn't Dad."

"Mom?"

"No, not my mom, either. It wasn't anybody."

"You mean, no one wrote in it? So why'd you call?"

"No, someone did write in it."

"So who?"

"I don't know."

"The cam didn't catch them?"

"It did catch them."

"But you don't know who it is?"

"That's what I'm saying."

"Ohmygod, someone broke into your house? Was it a guy?"

"No. I still don't know who it was."

"What, did he wear a hoodie? A ski mask?"

"No, no," Sam took a deep breath. "The camera shows the writing, but not the writer. It's like an invisible person is writing it."

"No way!"

"I am so not lying to you, Hailey."

"You are so messing with my head, aren't you?"

"No! Look, I can prove it. I have it on tape. Or drive, or whatever."

Hailey said, "I'm there," and hung up.

*****

The tap on her window by a flawlessly filed and buffed—but unpolished—fingernail announced the arrival of Hailey.

Sam closed her bedroom door and went to the window, lifting it up.

Hailey stepped through from the tree and started wiggling her fingers.

"Gimme, gimme," she said.

Sam handed her the diary.

June 16, 1914 6:37 p.m.

Who is Sam? I do not know a Sam. Yet, some Sam is writing in my diary. My personal diary!

I thought my method of hiding it was elaborate enough to fool Mr. Holmes. I even used a trick of his to see if my hiding place would be found. I licked a short hair I pulled from my brush and placed it across the tiny break so that I could see if it was disturbed. The hair remained, yet someone... Some Sam! ...still scribbled in my diary. Did they notice the hair and lick it themselves, putting it back exactly where I had? It seems so.

Whoever you are, you Sam, stop this at once!

"Okay, that's weird, just like before."

"Weirder," Sam said. "Wait 'til you see the video."

The girls shared the chair in front of the computer as Sam moved the slider back to where the writing started.

"Watch this."

As before, the writing crawled across the page like ants marching on a mission. Hailey's jaw dropped. When the writing got to the part where it disappeared under the pen that was laying on the page, she gasped. Her fingers went to her face as she said, "Ohmygod! Ohmygod! Ohmygod!"

Seeing it again startled Sam almost as much as it had the first time. Hailey's reaction proved she wasn't seeing things. It was really, really happening. Had happened.

"The smear in the ink?"

"What about it?" Sam asked.

"It's not there in the movie."

"I smeared it when I picked up the pen."

"It was wet!?"

"Yeah, it was creepy that…"

"You *have* to write back!"

"What are you talking about?"

"Right now! If the ink was wet, that means someone had barely finished writing it. You have to write back!"

Sam stared at Hailey, trying to let her brain catch up.

"Sam! Write back this instant, or I'll do it myself."

"No you won't! It's my crappy diary."

"Then do it. Pick up your pen and write."

Sam frowned. "What do I say?"

"Duh! Write stuff like, 'Hey, who are you?' 'Who is Holmes?' or 'Who is Palmer?'"

"We know who Holmes is."

"We do?"

"Yes, Sherlock."

"Don't tease me," Hailey said. "Who is it?"

"Sherlock Holmes. He was always doing that detective stuff like licking hairs and putting them on doors."

Hailey considered that. "Palmer, then. Find out who Palmer is. Crap, find out who anybody is!"

Sam scooted her corner of the chair closer to where the diary was. She picked up the pen and put it to the paper. Her hands trembled. In what was possibly her worst penmanship ever, she wrote:

June 16, 2013. 7:28 pm

Dear diary:

"Come on, get to it," Hailey said.

So, I don't get this, either. Who are you? Who's writing in this diary?—besides me, of course.

"Ask them to describe themselves," Hailey said.

I said that I'm Sam. What's your name?

"Good," Hailey said. "Ask them where they live or something."

I live in a little town called Fremont. Where do you live?

"No, you're sounding like you're pen pals," said Hailey.

"You wanted me to ask."

"Yeah, okay. Move it along."

I wonder who you are and it sounds like you wonder who I am. You say you wonder if someone is playing a trick on you. I'm doing the writing, but I'm not playing a trick. Are you playing one on me?

Oh, and who is "Palmer?"

"That's good," said Hailey. "Maybe you should put a smiley face on it."

"A smiley? You've got to be kidding."

"To show you're friendly. This is like a ghost or something."

Sam wrote another line.

Hope you're not a ghost.

She drew a little circle and added pinpoint eyes and a smile. Then, they waited.

They cruised Facebook together, checking every few seconds to see if anything appeared on the diary page. They looked at Pinterest, and the diary. They chatted. They looked at the diary.

After about an hour, Hailey said, "I've got to get home. I left without saying where I was going."

"I thought maybe we'd see the writing happen," Sam said.

Hailey laughed. "Me, too. I would have peed my pants!"

"Exactly!" said Sam.

They spent another moment looking at the diary. Then, Hailey said, "Got to go. Hey, why don't I put the diary in the Library on my way out?"

"Why?"

Hailey shrugged, "I don't know. If I hide it even you wouldn't know where it is. Maybe whoever is doing this is watching you hide it."

"Right. And then they become invisible when they write in it."

"I'm just sayin'. It might make it tougher for them to find it."

"Yeah, maybe," Sam said. "So we'd be, like, doing an experiment?"

Hailey nodded.

"Then take it home with you."

Hailey straightened up. "Home? Me?"

"It writes, but it doesn't bite."

"Sounds like a slogan," Hailey said. "Get the Crappy Used Diary. It writes, but it doesn't bite!"

Sam laughed. "So, will you?"

"Take it home? Uh, I guess."

JUNE 2014

Sunday	Monday	Tuesday	Wednesday	Thursday	Friday	Saturday
1	2	3	4	5	6	7
8	9	10	11	12	13	14
15 B Day!	16	17	18	19	20	21
22	23	24	25	26	27	28
29	30					

The next day as Sam watched through her kitchen window, Hailey came riding down the gravel drive like biker zombies were after her. She didn't bother knocking on the kitchen door.

"Your room," Hailey said, already headed there.

Sam trotted to catch up.

When they were in Sam's room, with the door closed behind them, Hailey slipped out of her backpack, retrieved the diary, and threw it on the bed.

"So, what's up?" Sam asked.

"Open it."

Hailey shoved her fingers into her jeans front pocket and started fishing something out. Sam opened the diary.

"Hey, it's all torn!"

"Only one page," Hailey said.

Sam ran her finger along the inside spine. On the left were the entries from the night before. On the right was a blank page. In the center was the ragged remnant of a page.

"You mean someone tore a page out while you had it?"

"No, I did that."

"You tore my diary?"

"What do you care? You hate it, don't you?"

"Yeah, but..."

"Never mind! That's not the important part. Well it is, I guess."

Hailey unfolded a piece of paper she'd retrieved from her pocket.

"Here it is."

Sam took it from her and smoothed it out on the duvet on her bed. The paper was not only wrinkled, it showed creases from folding and a couple dozen little holes.

"This is a mess."

"That's on purpose," Hailey said.

"And this is the page you tore out?"

Hailey nodded.

"There's more writing on it."

"Yeah, I sorta noticed that."

"They wrote in it even at your house?"

"Yes, yes, but that's still not the important part."

"But why'd you tear it out?"

"*That's* the important part," Hailey said. "I thought it would be a better experiment if I tore out a page."

"What difference..."

"A *blank* page."

Sam stared at her, then dropped her eyes to the crumpled paper.

"It's not blank."

"Not anymore," Hailey said, beaming. "We've caught a ghost!"

Sam skimmed over the new entry on the rumpled page, not really reading it.

"There's more," Hailey said. "See all those holes?"

"Sure, what made them?"

"Staples. I tore out the page, folded it over and over until I was afraid it would get too thick. Then I stapled it shut, like a dozen times. After that, I slept with it under my pillow. When I got up this morning I pried all the staples out and," she waved her hand in a flourish toward the page, "this was there. The writing." Hailey gave a sharp nod as if that settled everything. "See? We've caught a ghost!"

***

Together, they read through the entry on the rumpled sheet for the fourth time.

June 17, 1914, early morning

I don't know what to say. I have hidden this oh so carefully and in different places. No matter what I do, someone... You? You say your name is Sam. If that is true, then you are someone I do not know. I do not know any boy named Sam.

You asked my name. This is my diary but, you are right, my name is not in here. My name is Emma Rose Reed.

Is this my diary? Father gave it to me. It must be so. Yet, you write as if it is your diary & that your father gave it to you. That is not possible.

Fremont is a town not six miles from my home. If that is where you live, I must look for some Sam.

You asked who Palmer is. The Palmer Method, I meant. It's not as if I know him.

And, what is that little sketch supposed to be? It looks like a sun with a face. Is that supposed to be you?

What else can I say? This feels so silly.

I am 14 years old. My date of birth was June 12, 1900, just at the turn of the century. I live on a farm along the Bannock River. I like cats. And I cannot do this! I fear you are the devil himself! Be gone, you Sam!

"It has to be my dad," Sam said.

"How?"

"I don't know. Look at what it says." Sam started making points on her fingers. "First, this Emma person has my last name. Second, she lives in a farm house six miles from Fremont. That's got to be the Big House. Third, I think she's talking about hiding the diary in the place where Dad found it."

"And four," said Hailey. "She's got nearly your same birthday."

"Exactly! That's a dead giveaway, because it was a birthday present. Plus, she thinks I'm a boy. Dad always calls me Sammy and teases me about Sam being a boy's name."

Hailey frowned. "I still don't see how he's doing it."

"Maybe he's got a camera, too. I mean, we used a camera to try to catch whoever was writing it. Maybe he has a camera set up so he can see where we're hiding it."

"He has a camera in my bedroom?" Hailey asked.

That didn't seem likely. What it did seem was really,

really creepy.

"Maybe *your* parents are in on it."

"Your dad hardly knows my parents."

"Still, maybe."

"Okay, but how did he make himself invisible to write in it?"

Sam was quick to answer. "Special effects! They do a lot harder stuff than that in the movies."

"Does your dad know how to do special effects?"

Sam hesitated. "Not really. I had to show him how to use the camera on his phone."

Their eyes fell back to the paper.

Hailey snorted. "She thinks you're the devil."

"Ha, ha. And, we think she's a ghost."

"Or your dad."

"Yeah, it's got to be Dad."

"Still..."

"Still, what?"

"If it really is some girl from a hundred years ago, we could really mess with her."

"It's Dad, but what do you mean?"

"Well, we could tell her what the weather was going to be like the next day, for one thing."

"We could?"

"Sure. The net has all kinds stuff like that. She was complaining about the rain. You can look it up. Even better, we could tell her what was going to happen in the news before it happened." Hailey's eyes got big. "We could predict the future!"

"She'd think I'm the devil for sure."

"It'd be fun! Let's try it."

Hailey slid into Sam's computer chair, taking up about half the seat on the right and leaving a space next to her for Sam.

"What's the date?"

"Today?"

"No, three weeks from Tuesday. Of course, today."

When Hailey moved the mouse there was the nearly inaudible crackle of a screen coming to life.

"Never mind. It's June 17. Now, let's see what happened on June 17, 1914."

Typing in What happened on June 17, 1914, Hailey hit return. The first entry was for a Wikipedia page apparently devoted to questions about days in history.

"Vlad the Impaler tried to assassinate some dude named Mehmed. That was in 1462, though. Hey, here's an Idaho entry, Hailey said "The Battle of Whitebird Hill. Crap, that was in 1877."

"There's nothing for 1914," said Sam.

"Doesn't matter. We're doing it wrong, anyway," Hailey said "We want to predict something a few days in the future."

On the right side of the screen was a calendar. Hailey clicked on the 18th, found nothing for 1914, then clicked to 19, 20, and all the way through to June 23 before finding an entry.

"'Mexican Revolution: Pancho Villa takes—how do you pronounce that?" asked Hailey, pointing to the screen.

"Zack-kat-is? I don't know. Would she know about that?"

"Probably. I've heard of Pancho Villa and I don't know squat about history."

"But, would it be in the paper right away?"

"Why wouldn't it?"

"It's not like today. They didn't have, like, instant communication. They didn't have the internet."

"Duh. Or TV, even. I know that. They had phones, though." Hailey frowned. "Didn't they?"

Hailey turned around and Googled "telephone invented." Another Wikipedia entry gave her the answer.

"See, 1875. They had phones by 1914, even in Fremont."

"Maybe."

Not completely satisfied with Pancho Villa, Hailey went back to clicking through dates.

"Here!"

"What?"

"This assassination. On June 28, 1914, Franz Ferdinand, the Archduke of Austria was assassinated. Remember that?"

"How could I remember that? I wasn't exactly alive back then."

"From history! That's what started World War One."

"Uh, sorta. I didn't remember the date."

"Who remembers dates? That would be important, though. It had to be important enough to be in all the papers if it's what started the war, right?"

"Probably. So, now what? We predict the start of World War One and that's supposed to impress my dad, how, exactly?"

"Not your dad. Emma."

"Serious?"

"Why not? It'll prove you're not the devil."

"Or, it'll prove I am the devil. It'd be like magic to her."

"Yeah," Hailey said. "But, at least she'd believe you're real."

"I don't care! She's the one who isn't real."

"So make her prove she is."

"How?"

They sat there at the computer a few more minutes, Hailey clicking through more dates. There was another assassination the next day that they didn't remember reading about. Some days didn't have a lot of entries. On some days, there was so much history they had to scroll down to find 1914. On July 4, the Archduke was buried.

"Killed his wife, too," Hailey said. "I didn't remember that."

On July 28, Austria-Hungry declared war on Serbia.

"That must have been the start of it," Sam said. "When did the US get into it?"

Hailey rattled the keyboard, and said, "Not until April 6, 1917."

"She might not believe us that killing the Archduke would mean a war."

Hailey shrugged. "Doesn't matter. If we predict the assassination, she'll be impressed enough."

"Uh, huh. That's what I want to do, impress the invisible girl who is really my dad."

"Or, who is really an invisible girl. You saw the writing. And, don't say it was your dad and his genius for special effects."

Sam got up off the chair and dropped backward onto her bed.

"This is so stupid! Why is he doing this?"

"Maybe he's not."

"Really? You think it's some kind of magic?"

"It'd be cool if it was, wouldn't it?"

Sam didn't answer. Of course, it would be cool. Who wouldn't want a little magic in their lives? Sam had long ago put magic up on the shelf with Santa, the tooth fairy, and the Easter Bunny. They were kid things. She wasn't a kid.

"Look, we have to try to figure it out. So, you have to write in it again."

"No I don't."

"You have to."

"You write in it if you're so hot for it."

Hailey said, "But, it's your diary."

"So what? It's not like I even like it. And, everybody else writes in it, anyway. Dad, the invisible girl."

"You really wouldn't mind?"

"Knock yourself out."

***

Hailey remembered to look up Palmer Method before she started. It was a way of teaching people penmanship.

"Must really work," Sam said.

"Worked for her, I guess," said Hailey. "She'll think I missed the lesson."

June 17, later the same day only a hundred years later

Hi! I'm not Sam. My name is Hailey and I'm Sam's friend. You should know that Sam isn't a boy, though it is kind of a boy's name, I guess. It's short for Samantha. And, guess what? She has the same last name as you, Reed. Cool, huh?

Sam doesn't think you exist. I kind of don't, either, but maybe I think it a little more than she does. She thinks you're her dad. That doesn't sound right. She thinks her dad is pretending to be you, Emma.

We've hid this diary in a couple of different places and someone keeps finding it and writing in it. We've even taken a picture of it with a webcam, and we could see the writing happen. It was awesome!

And, BTW, your writing is really cool. It's the best I've ever seen.

So, what else? Oh, Sam was born nearly the same day as you. Only in 2000, of course. She thinks you must live in an old house her dad is fixing up. Must have lived there, I mean. I suppose by now you're dead. Sorry about that. No one lives to be 114, though, do they?

We have something to tell you that will make you believe we are not the devil. Maybe. We live in 2014, and you say you live in 1914, so we're not the devil. Just girls in the future. Your future. So, we kinda know what is going to happen in your future, because to us it's the past. Does that make sense?

Anyway, the thing that is going to happen in your future is that an Archduke named Ferdinhand is going to be killed.

That will happen on June 28, 1914 over in Europe. It's going to start a war. The United States won't get involved in that war until 1917, but by then it will be a world war. The first one. There's a second one later, but don't worry about that yet.

And, the reason I'm writing on this page, instead of right beneath where you last wrote is because we tore the page where you wrote out of the book. The diary, I mean. It's still there in 1914, I suppose, but trust me. Here in 2014, it's a wad of paper.

That's probably enough for now.

Hey, one more thing! Think of a way you can prove to us that you're real, okay? Bye!

***

They spent most of the morning experimenting with the makeup. It was messy, but it worked. Once they got a pile of burnt almond about the size of a quarter, they were able to mix the oil with it until it was just the right consistency. Almost the right consistency. The first time they tried it, it dripped down Hailey's face and made her look like she had black tears. They made up a little more "coal" and added it to the mess.

"Hey, not bad," Sam said.

"Am I beautiful?" Hailey asked, batting her eyes.

"You look like a raccoon. It's so you."

Hailey examined herself in the mirror. "That'll work. Mascara?"

So, they made up another batch of almond coal. This time, they mixed a drop of honey with it, then added another tiny drop. Hailey had a mascara applicator they had stolen from Rachel the winter before. She swirled it around in the black paste until there was a thin coat on the brush.

Mouth agape, Hailey brushed the substance into her eyelashes. It darkened them and made them stick together two or three at a time.

"Cool!" Sam said. "And when you get tired of it, you can wet your fingers, pull it off and eat it."

"Gross."

***

At about 12:30 they broke away from the cosmetics experiment and threw together some cheese sandwiches for lunch. After they were done they went to check on the diary. This time they hid it in plain sight, tucked between a couple of books on one of Sam's shelves.

Though they half expected to find another entry, seeing the words written there gave each of them a thrill.

June 17, 1914. Another entry

This is a game of some sort. Someone has given me a mystery to solve, maybe because I adore the books of Mr. Doyle.

For now, I choose to believe that. The Devil wouldn't have such terrible penmanship and would surely know better than to say he had "hid" this diary. If the Dark One has been with us for all of human history, he must have picked up the rules of grammar. And, perhaps in your world Ferdinand is spelled with an "h." In mine, that is not the case. Also, I think things are not nearly as cool in my world as you seem to think. It has been raining, but it has also been rather warm and muggy.

So, to play along...

Please tell me what a "webcam" is and what BTW is.

*You speak of wars where the whole world takes part. That
makes me consider the Devil, again. Who else could cause such
a thing? And you will predict them? Some future person could,
if they knew history. I put myself in that place and realize I
could tell someone in 1860 that the war between the states
was about to happen. Getting them to believe me would be the
challenge.*

*You say that is your challenge with me. So, <u>to play along</u>,
I will read the newspapers for the days after June 28 to see if
there is mention of your "Ferdinhand."*

*You give me a challenge of my own. I am to prove to you
that I am real.*

*I have put on the hat of Holmes & I think I have a way to
test this. I will do something this very day that will prove you
a trickster, I think! You "Sam" girl; you "Hailey." I have heard
those names before, the first for a boy or man, the second for
a small town in Idaho. You say you are neither of those, but a
girl—two girls. Well, we will see what the jar says.*

"What does she mean 'we'll see what the jar says?'"
Hailey asked.

"Who knows? Maybe its something like a Ouija board,
or maybe one of those magic eight balls."

"A magic jar?"

"So, look it up." Sam gave an absent wave toward the
computer.

Hailey sat down in front of the monitor and typed in
"magic jar." In a second, more than 9 million results came
back. She skimmed the first few.

"Ha!"

"What?"

"We may have her! Well, or him. Whoever it is," said Hailey. "There's all kinds of worthless stuff here, but most of the pages have something to do with the Legend of Zelda."

Sam frowned. "Isn't that a computer game, or something?"

"I think so. It's one of those where you journey someplace looking for a magic whatever. Along the way you pick up swords and stuff. Magic jars are one of the things you pick up."

"How would someone in 1914 know about a computer game?"

"Exactly! I think they screwed up. We can call them on that."

Sam did not look convinced. "If that's even what they mean."

"Well, it's worth a try. We can ask them about Zelda and see what they say."

"Okay. Do you want to write that?"

Hailey's left leg bounced up and down while Sam waited for her reply.

"Nah. You go ahead. It's your diary. Besides, she thinks I'm a moron."

"She didn't say that."

"No, but she doesn't like my grammar and the way I spell."

Sam scooted so that her back was against the wall while she sat on her bed and began to write.

June 17, 2014, again. Now about 1 in the afternoon.

So, this is Sam. You wanted to know what a webcam is.

"How do I explain a webcam to her?"

Hailey replied, "Tell her it's like a movie camera."

"Will she know what a movie is?"

"Sure. She talked about somebody going to see a movie."

"Yeah, but she didn't call it a 'movie'."

"What did she call it?"

"Nothing, really. She just said the name of it. We figured out it was a movie. But movies were brand new, then. I'm not sure they called them movies."

Hailey said, "Maybe not. Try motion picture."

"How about moving picture?"

"Even better."

"They had cameras, right? Can you look that up?"

"I already know they had cameras. They had pictures of the Civil War."

"Oh, right. And, I guess they'd have cameras if they had movies. Duh."

A webcam is like a moving picture camera.

"Wait, how do I explain the Internet?"

Hailey shrugged. "Don't. It's too complicated. Just leave it at camera."

You also asked about BTW. Those are initials that mean By The Way. We use initials when we text write to each other sometimes.

So, does the magic jar have something to do with Zelda?

Sam couldn't think of what else to say. Finally, she

wrote:

Do you have cars back then?

When she was finished, Sam turned the diary to Hailey, who quickly read the entry.

"'Do you have cars back then?' That is so lame!"

"Well, I just wondered."

"Of course they had cars." Hailey's brow wrinkled. "I think." She slid off the bed and headed for the computer.

After a few keystrokes, she said, "Sure. They were invented in the 1880s. Maybe they called them horseless carriages, or something, but they had them."

The rest of the afternoon they hung out, often peeking at the diary to see if anything else appeared. It did not.

Nothing appeared that evening, either.

At 10:30 that night Hailey texted.

Anythin?

Nope.

May b busy.

Whateves

Sleep on it

Under pillow.

JUNE 2014

Sunday	Monday	Tuesday	Wednesday	Thursday	Friday	Saturday
1	2	3	4	5	6	7
8	9	10	11	12	13	14
15 *B Day!*	16	17	18	19	20	21
22	23	24	25	26	27	28 *Duke Dies*
29	30					

When Sam woke up at about 8:30, she checked the diary through bleary eyes.

June 18, 1914, 6 am

It is done.

First, get a shovel. Do you still have shovels there in the future? Or, do you have magic fairies do your digging?

And, I must say, I was not the one who said anything about a magic jar. It is a simple jar. There is nothing magical about it (and who is Zelda?).

Once you have your shovel you will need to dig. If my home is the house your dad "is fixing up," then you will be able to go to the northeast corner of the house. Dig down right next to the foundation at that corner. An inch or two beneath the ground you will find a flat river rock. Lift that up and dig around with your fingers until you find the jar I buried there. Inside the jar is a message I left for you.

Once you find the message, write it in this diary. If the

message is correct, then maybe I will believe you!

PS: We do not have a car. My Aunt Clarice and Uncle Walter have a Model T. Do you have a car?

Sam read it three times, then pulled out her phone. Hailey had texted her earlier, but she must have slept through the buzz.

U up?

Getting no reply, Hailey had sent one more.

Text when alive.

Sam put her thumbs to work.

Up. New wrds. Come whn can.

***

"That's like six miles," Hailey said.

"It's paved most of the way. We can do it."

"Not carrying a shovel on a bike, we can't. Are you sure there aren't tools there?"

"Maybe. Dad's been working on the inside, mostly."

"Does your mom have one of those little shovel thingies? Like, for planting flowers?"

"A trowel?"

"Yeah, whatever they are," Hailey said.

"I think I could find one. That'd be better than nothing."

Sam found a couple of trowels in the garage and borrowed one. It went into a small backpack along with the diary and a couple of sack lunches her mother had insisted on making.

"You'll need your energy. The Big House is out there a ways."

The girls said it wasn't necessary, but put up little resistance. A sandwich wasn't really such a bad idea. They'd each take a water bottle, too.

"Glad to see you're taking an interest," Mrs. Reed called to them as they started to pedal away.

"Just something to do," Sam called back. She was so not taking an interest in that old house.

The first five miles was an easy ride, taking them less than half an hour. The sky was mostly clear and the morning was cool. They barely worked up a sweat.

The last mile was gravel. Chipped gravel would have been difficult with bike tires. This was worse. It was gravel straight out of some gravel pit. The rocks were three to six inches across. They seemed designed to impede their progress rather than make it easier. The last mile or so took them another half hour, with frequent stops to put a foot down to regain balance.

When they finally arrived they were hot and thirsty. The girls dropped their bikes on the tall grass of what once was a front lawn. They sat under a big pine and broke into the sandwiches.

Her mouth half full, Sam said, "So which way is north? I can't ever remember directions."

Hailey thumbed back over her shoulder. "That way."

"Really? The river always confuses me. On a map it runs mostly east to west across the state. I know that where we live it runs north and south, but I still get confused."

Hailey swallowed some sandwich and took a sip of water.

"We're looking at the northeast corner of the house right there." She nodded across the lawn. "It's behind that bush."

"Let's check it out."

Both girls left their lunches behind, ignoring apples Sam's mother had included. They got down on their knees and looked into the shadow behind the bush.

"Smells nice," Hailey said.

"Lilacs. This would have been pretty a week or so ago. Not much left, now."

Hailey pushed some lower branches out of her way, breaking a couple.

"Be careful," said Sam.

"I'm fine."

"I meant with the bush. We don't want to kill it."

"You couldn't kill it with a tank. It's almost as tall as the house."

Hailey squinted at the foundation of the house where it disappeared into the dirt.

"Nobody's been digging lately. It's all dry and hard back here." She wiggled her fingers behind her. "Gimme the thingy."

"Trowel!"

"Towel, trowel. Whatever."

Sam handed it to her and Hailey began to dig. The ground was hard but each thrust brought away about a handful of dirt.

"I thought she said the rock was a couple inches down."

Sam said, "Let me check." She pulled out the diary, ran

her finger across the latest entry, and said, "Yeah, one or two inches."

"Well, I'm down about four and..."

The trowel hit something hard.

"There's something. I think it's a rock, but it's about six inches deep."

"Can you get it out?"

"I'm trying."

Sam could see Hailey's arms working away at something and heard a series of scrapes.

After a few minutes of that, Hailey backed out. "You try it," she said. "My arms are getting tired."

Sam crawled beneath the bush. Hailey had uncovered a good sized river rock, bigger even than those they'd fought through on the road.

"One thing's for sure," Hailey said. "No one has buried anything there recently. But, why is it so deep?"

"Could be just a rock. I mean, not the rock she was talking about," Sam said. "I think it would be deeper than she said, though. The ground grows."

"What? You've got to be kidding. You think the ground grows?"

"Yeah. At least, a lawn gets higher. Dad made me help him edge the lawn last summer along the curb. He told me you have to do that because the dead grass gets all matted and builds up. New grass grows on top of that. Every year your lawn builds up a little more dirt."

"This isn't in the lawn, though."

"Well, it probably was once. I don't know, but I think

dirt builds up a little everywhere. That's why they call them archaeological digs, right?"

Hailey was quiet for a moment.

"So, this is like an archaeological dig?"

"Kind of. Hey, I think I got it!"

Sam used the trowel to pry against the rock. It came loose and she was able to get her fingers under it. She passed the rock back to Hailey, who started brushing it off. Meanwhile, Sam stuck her fingers into the dirt looking for the jar.

"Ow! Son of a..."

Sam backed out from beneath the bush and turned around, shaking one hand.

"Something bit me," she said.

"Oh my god! Are you hurt?"

Sam brushed her hands together and examined her finger tips. There was a bright red spot of blood on the tip of one.

"Looks more like a cut," Hailey said. She crawled back behind the bush.

After a moment, she too backed out.

"Here's your biter." Hailey held up a triangle of light blue glass. Sam took it from her.

"Crap, I'll probably get lockjaw, or something."

"What?"

"Lockjaw," Sam said. "You know, the thing you can get from rusty nails and stuff."

"There's more, I think," Hailey said, shuffling back into the space behind the lilac.

After a little more digging, Hailey asked Sam to get her one of the used baggies from lunch. She began putting glass shards into it.

"Be careful," Sam said. "Don't cut yourself." She did not say what she was thinking, which was that she, Sam, had at least had all her shots. Lockjaw—wasn't it really called tetanus?—wasn't a real worry. Hailey had never had vaccinations. Cuts could be more serious for her.

"Here's most of it," Hailey said, handing Sam about three quarters of a broken blue jar. "The top of it still has part of the lid on." She backed out with a gray cap in her hand. The ring of it still held the jagged neck of the jar.

"I wonder why it didn't rust," Hailey said.

Sam glanced at the broken bottle top. She was more interested in the larger piece that was still intact. In raised letters across the front of the broken jar it said "Ball." The word was at an angle and underlined. Below that were the words "Perfect Mason."

"Kind of a pretty color," said Hailey. All the glass was a light blue. "Is there anything in it?"

"Dirt," Sam replied. She dumped the contents onto a bare patch beneath the lilac, then smoothed her finger through it. There was a scrap of paper. Two scraps.

Excited, Hailey said, "Is that it?"

Sam looked at both sides of both pieces of paper. "No writing."

Hailey's shoulders slumped. "You sure? Let me see."

The scraps were nearly dust. They broke apart in her fingers with the slightest touch. If there had been writing there, it had faded years ago, maybe decades ago.

"Still, there was a jar there, like she said."

"Yeah," Sam said, with little enthusiasm.

"Doesn't that prove it?"

"How? There wasn't a note."

"There was paper. Sorta. Maybe there was a note once."

"Yeah, maybe. That's hardly proof."

"But, somebody buried the jar," Hailey said. "And, it was a long time ago, not, like, yesterday."

Sam sighed. "I guess. I was just hoping for proof, one way or another."

"Well, your dad didn't bury it."

"Probably not. I don't think he's even been out here for a few days."

"Days? This has been buried for years. The dirt was like a concrete sidewalk over the top of it."

"I know, but one thing bothers me," Sam said. "If it's been buried for, like, a hundred years, why isn't the lid rusty?"

Hailey looked closely at the fragment of jar that still held the metal ring. It was a dull gray.

"There's some rust," Hailey said. "Look here, where it's scratched. That part's rusted clear through. And it looks like the flat part rusted away completely."

The ring of the two-part lid was almost intact. Only traces of the flat disc that went across the jar's top were left. Rusty traces.

"I wonder what broke it," Hailey said.

"Frost," said Sam. "If the dirt got wet, then froze, it

could break the jar."

The girls sat there on the ground. After a moment, Hailey looked at the house and asked, "Can we go inside?"

"What for?"

"I don't know. I'd like to see it."

"It's just an old house."

"Yeah, but it's the house she lived in," Hailey said, then added, "If she exists, I mean."

"Exist-*ed*," said Sam. "She's supposed be dead, you know."

"Anyway, I want to see it. Do you have a key?"

"No, but I know where Dad keeps it."

They passed between two thin, ornately carved pillars to get to the front door. The paint was chipped and peeling. On one of them, someone—probably Sam's dad—had started scraping away the paint and exposing the wood beneath it. He hadn't gotten very far. The head of a lion, about four inches high, guarded the house a couple feet from the bottom of the post. Three of its mates gave silent roars from the other three sides. The paint was gone from the flat surfaces below all four lions, but only one of them showed any sign of scraping. Little bits of hard paint remained in most of the folds of its mane. Sam ran her fingers over the exposed wood and up across the lion's nose. It would take a lot of work to get that paint out.

The key was on top of a window frame next to the front door. Sam couldn't reach it. They found an old battered bucket to give her the extra foot she needed.

In the movies, opening an old, old door was always

accompanied by the sound effect of prolonged creaking. It was the cue for haunted houses. This door opened without a sound, swinging on its hinges as if they were new that day.

"This is the hall," Sam said.

"No duh."

Sam gave Hailey a little back-handed hit on the shoulder.

"The kitchen is at the end and the bedrooms are on the right."

"What's the door to the left?" Hailey asked.

"Kind of a living room. It connects to the kitchen."

They took a few steps down the hall.

"Whoa! Look at this!"

Hailey was pointing at a huge map mounted on the wall between the bedroom doors. It was a map of the United States.

"Yeah, my great-great—maybe three greats—grandfather put that up the year he built the house."

"Wow, when was that?"

"I don't remember. I think there's a date on the map someplace." Sam pointed to the lower right. "There."

Hailey leaned down and squinted at the legend in the corner of the map. "United States and Territories with Adjacent Parts of Canada and Mexico," she read. "Also part of the West Indian Islands, blah, blah... There! 1887! So, this house was built in 1887?"

Sam shrugged. "I think so. Dad says the map was new when the house was built."

"That is so old!"

"Yeah, I suppose."

Sam started down the hall toward the kitchen.

"Wait!," Hailey said. "I want to see Idaho."

"It's in the upper left…"

"I know where it is," Hailey said, moving her finger across the map to the Pacific Northwest.

"Actually, you're not supposed to touch it."

"Oh, sorry," Hailey said.

"The oil from your fingers isn't good for it."

"My fingers aren't oily."

"Fingerprints. They're oil. Everybody leaves fingerprints."

"Right. Hey, it doesn't have Fremont on here."

"It probably wasn't even a town back then. Or, maybe it was too small."

"There's a town called Presto," Hailey said. "Where's that?"

"Here, actually," Sam said. "This little valley is called Presto. It was named after the first man who homesteaded here."

"Homesteaded?"

"You know. Like, the government gave away land if you would build a house and farm it. We learned that in fourth grade or something."

"Okay, but where's the town?"

"There wasn't a town. Only a bunch of farms. Presto was really just a post office and the post office was here."

"Here?"

"Here, here. In this house."

"A house was a post office?"

"Not the whole house," Sam said. "It was just a bureau, or whatever you call it. A piece of furniture. I can show you if you want."

"Yeah."

Sam opened the door on the left, to what she had called the living room. This door did creak, as if the house protested the intrusion.

"That's it, in the corner," Sam said.

The "post office" bureau was about the size of a dresser. Instead of a mirror it had a tall cabinet set back from the front edge of the piece. There were shelves and nooks where one might keep office supplies.

"This is the post office part," Sam said, reaching up and flipping up a narrow door that ran all the way along the top of the cabinet. When open, it revealed half a dozen little boxes. Over the top of each box, on the underside of the door, was lettering, A to F, G to K and so on.

"My great-grandmother was the postmistress," Sam said. "Or maybe great-great. I never can remember the right number of greats."

"Can I touch it?" Hailey asked.

"Sure, I guess. Dad hasn't ever said not to."

Hailey ran her fingers across the surface of the wood and reached up to feel one of the boxes.

"And this is how they got mail in 1887? They all came to this house?"

Sam shrugged. "This is where they came."

"So, somebody from a bigger post office would bring all

the mail here, and your grandmother would sort it, right?"

"Great-grandmother. Or two greats, but yeah."

"That is so cool!"

Hailey's reaction surprised Sam. Nothing ever impressed Hailey, unless it was makeup or a hot boy.

There were stacks of old letters jammed into the alphabetized compartments. Hailey touched some. "Can I?"

"I suppose. Put them back where you found them."

Hailey began sorting through the envelopes, taking the top one off and putting it to the back, reading the return addresses as she went.

"These aren't in the right place."

"What do you mean?"

"This is G through K, but they're all random."

Sam pulled out the stack from A through F. She found a letter from a Mrs. Brower and a John Firth. None of the rest were A through F.

"Well, it's been, like, a hundred years since it was a post office," Sam said. "These are probably just old letters stuffed in here to save them. I don't think anyone ever threw anything away."

"Some of these are really old. This one's 1942," Hailey said. "Oh, and here's one from 1918."

"I wonder if any of the stamps are valuable," Sam said. She hadn't thought of that before. "I guess we could ask Beaker."

Hailey frowned. "Why Beaker?"

The man's name was Baker, but most of the science class called him Beaker, maybe because he had a big nose.

Maybe because he used beakers in class sometimes, but probably because his hair was frizzy and his glasses made his eyes a little buggy and reminded someone, sometime of a certain Muppet.

"He collects stamps."

"Why?"

"I don't know. It's his hobby, I guess. He's a geek, right?"

"Totally. Not to mention, old."

"Dad and I went over to his place once. He was selling a lathe or a saw or some kind of power thingy Dad wanted. While we were there, he wanted to show Dad his stamp collection."

"Astounding," Hailey said.

"I know, right? He had hundreds of them all perfect in plastic binders. He showed us some that were worth more than a thousand dollars."

"Stamps?"

"Rare stamps."

"Like, what makes them rare?"

"I don't know. They're old? There aren't many of them left?"

"There's a ton of old ones right here," Hailey said. "Maybe we're millionaires!"

"No, these have been used. They have to be new stamps."

"New old stamps? How is that even possible?"

"Well, not new, but not used, either. You can't just peel them off an old envelope." Sam held one of the envelopes up. "And look at the post mark."

"So?"

"It kind of ruins the stamp when there's ink on it."

Her dreams of being a millionaire dashed, Hailey stuffed the old envelopes back in the desk. She took letters out of the next cubbyhole and started flipping through them. About halfway through, she stopped.

"Holy shit!"

"What?"

"It's her! Ghost girl!"

Hailey shoved the letter toward Sam who took it from her. The letter was addressed to Emma Rose Reed. The postmark was November 14, 1912.

"This was written before she started the diary," Sam said.

"See if the handwriting matches!"

"What?" Sam threw Hailey a withering look. "It's to her, not from her, stupid."

"Oh, yeah. Well, open it, anyway."

Sam squeezed the edges so the ragged end pooched open and worked a single page out of the envelope. She read out loud.

Dearest Cousin:

Are you recovered from your cold? They are the nastiest things, sometimes, aren't they?

I am doing well, though I hate the weather. I can rarely ride anymore because it is too slick or too sloppy. Peter Pan is such a shaggy mess, anyway. He looks like a big bear! I suppose your Wendy is the same. She is such a pretty thing. Give her a lump for me.

I do hope you can come for a visit in the summer. I miss my cuz! You really must plan to stay a whole week.

Oh, I have the newest Anne! It is called Anne of the Island. I have just started it and can hardly put it down to write to my favorite girl. You must get it.

Sorry to hear your mother is having her troubles, again. The poor dear. Give Aunt Ethel my best, and write again, soon??

Love,

Florence

Hailey took the page from Sam and skimmed over it.

"Not as good at writing as ghost girl."

"Better'n you."

"Better'n you, too. So, Florence is her friend. Her cousin."

"I guess," said Sam. "And Emma's mother's named Ethel."

"You sure? It says Aunt Ethel."

"Well, she'd be her cousin's aunt, right?"

"I guess. Not sure from the letter that she's talking about the same person."

Sam looked at the envelope, again. "1912. And it looks real."

"The letter?"

"Yeah, and the envelope. This isn't something someone planted here to fool us."

"So, ghost girl is real, right?" asked Hailey.

"I think so. It's just too weird."

"But we know more stuff, now. We know her name and we know her mother's name and her cousin's name. We could do the genealogy."

"The what?"

"Genealogy. You know, like a family tree. Find out who's related to who."

Sam did not seem as excited as Hailey thought she should be.

"Come on, Sam. We can figure out how ghost girl is related to you."

"But, how?"

"How? I'm kind of a Mormon, ya know?"

Sam's face was blank.

"Mormons do genealogy all the time so they can make sure they've baptized everyone and their dog so they'll all go to heaven."

"Mormon dogs go to heaven?"

"Not the dogs. Actually, I don't know about the dogs. I meant that Mormons get all obsessive about their relatives so they can be saved by baptism, even after they're dead."

"They baptize dead people?"

"Not like, bodies, or anything. Someone stands in for them."

"That's weird."

"Hey, I didn't say I believe all that. My parents do, though. My mom has our whole family figured out—the genealogy, I mean. She'd do yours, too, if we asked her. She'd probably have a heart attack because she'd think you were ready to convert."

"I'd need to be a Mormon? I don't think..."

"Nah, she'd help you anyway. She likes doing that stuff."

Hailey folded the letter and put it back into its envelope. She slid it into the back pocket of her jeans and raised her eyebrows in a silent question to Sam. Sam shrugged. It was just an old letter.

They spent the next few minutes exploring the house. The kitchen held a long, sturdy table so big it must have been built right inside the room. The cast iron wood-burning stove was too big to come through any door, but there it was hulking against an inside wall. Next to that was a bright red push-button range.

"Why two stoves?" Hailey asked.

"Dad's great aunt lived here before she died. She used the wood stove most of her life, but decided she wanted a new electric one."

"I've never seen a red one before."

"Dad says that's what she wanted, a bright red stove. They did weird colors in the 50s."

"She must have been a cool old lady."

The refrigerator stood on white metal legs. On the top of it was a round metal box attached with vents all around it. The sink was big and deep and white.

Hailey was trying all the doors and vents on the cast iron stove. Sam was bored.

"I'm going to go look in the bedrooms," Sam said.

Hailey followed her. The first bedroom was nothing special. There was a bed, a nightstand, and a dresser, along with a wooden armoire in the corner. All the walls were a solid color, a dirty white. The second bedroom was furnished about the same, though the walls were probably once yellow. There was also a big old radio sitting on a table in one corner, a braided, cloth-covered power cord dangling over the edge like a dejected tail.

"It must be in one of the upstairs bedrooms," Sam said.

"What are you looking for?"

"You'll see. C'mon."

Hailey followed Sam up the steep, narrow stairs from the hallway to the attic bedrooms. Each bedroom had a small window. The one on the right looked out from the side of the house. The bedroom on the left had a small dormer window sticking out from the roof. It was in this room that Sam found what she was looking for. This was the only one of the four that had wallpaper.

The wallpaper was cream colored with a light blue design. The pattern was a complex series of scenes. One showed a teenage boy on the back of a horse gesturing to a teenage girl who was in a full-length dress. At the girl's feet a toddler played on the ground. Another scene was of a boy hunting with a spear in his hand, which seemed out of place. The way they were all dressed, the figures looked like they might have lived in Europe a couple of centuries earlier. One boy was blowing through a decorated cow horn, while two dogs chased an extravagantly antlered deer. Scattered through the repeating scenes were grazing cows and leafy trees.

"Who picked out the hideous wallpaper?" Hailey asked.

"Really," said Sam. She looked along the bottom of the walls, then saw what she was looking for leaning up against the foot of a battered and dusty dresser.

"Here it is," she said, bending down. "This is where Dad found the diary." Sam looked under the dresser. "There's the opening, back there."

Hailey got down on her hands and knees.

"It's too dark to see anything," Hailey said. "Let's move the dresser."

They did, both getting grimy fingers as a result. When they knelt down by the hole, Hailey said, "Reach in there and see what you can find."

"You reach in. There's probably mice and spiders," Sam said. "I wish we had a light."

"So, we'll bring a flashlight next time."

Hailey lifted the wallpaper-covered board and fitted it into the hole.

"Wow. Perfect! All the pictures match up."

"You'd never see it under the dresser unless you were looking for it."

"And maybe not then," Hailey said. "How'd your Dad find it?"

"He didn't say. I suppose he was poking around to see what needed fixing."

Sam ran her fingers across the board and found the little finishing nail her dad had mentioned. Gripping it between her fingers she pulled. The board came right out.

Hailey took the wallpaper covered board from her.

"This kid on the horse needs a mustache," she said.

***

They rode back home with their lunch baggies in their backpacks full of broken glass, their inconclusive treasure. As they neared her house, Sam noticed a familiar little hatchback parked in the driveway. She heard the screen door slam and saw her sister step out onto the landing.

"Rachel!"

"Hey, Grub," the young woman said. "Just in time to help me haul some of this crap in."

Rachel was wearing flip-flops, jeans and a baggy men's shirt. This wasn't exactly the fashion sense Sam was used to seeing in her big sister. She was so totally together most of the time. The hatch was open on the old Toyota, revealing half a dozen boxes, a heaping laundry basket, and a backpack.

"Hey, dipwad," Rachel said, when she got close to Hailey.

"I'm not a dipwad."

"Sherpa, then," Rachel said, grabbing one strap of the backpack and tossing it in Hailey's direction.

"What, for free?" Hailey asked.

"Oh, you're a professional girl, now?"

Hailey reddened, but it didn't' slow her. "Sherpas don't work for free, either, Rach."

"Whatever." Rachel raised an eyebrow. "What do you charge, Sherpa?"

"Lip gloss!"

"Too much. I've got a half-full bottle of Galactic Moon Candy."

"Nail polish? Well..."

"Take or leave it."

"Take it! Do you need help with boxes, too?"

"That includes help with boxes, greedy butt."

Sam said, "I thought you weren't coming home until tomorrow."

Rachel shoved a box into her arms and said, "We got off the river a little early, so I came straight home." There was something about the way she said it that didn't seem quite right to Sam.

Rachel had gone with the university outdoor club on a week-long float on the Middle Fork of the Salmon River before coming home for the summer.

"Was it awesome?" Sam asked.

Before Rachel could answer, their mom called from the porch, "Need any help?"

"Nah, I've got the dipwads."

"Rachel!"

"Sherpas. I've got Sherpas."

In a low voice, Rachel said to Sam, "I'll tell you about it later."

Getting Rachel settled into her room took a few minutes. Sam wanted to ask her about the float, but their mom kept hanging around asking questions of her own, the answer to most of which was "fine." Finals, friends, float trip, the drive from Salmon, all of those were fine. Still her mother persisted. Sam finally gave up and slipped away to her room with Hailey.

There, they unpacked their prize. The girls laid out the

pieces of the jar next to the computer. There were eight of them, including the jagged mouth with the gray ring still twisted tight onto it.

"Let's glue it together," Hailey said.

"We should wash it first."

"Do you have good glue?"

"What's good?"

"I mean, do you have anything besides Elmer's?"

"I've got a glue stick."

"That won't work. We need something stronger."

"Super glue? Dad's got some in the shop."

"Perfect," Hailey said. "You go get it while I wash off the pieces."

After a few minutes of looking, Sam found a barely used tube of super glue in a small drawer in the work bench. She made a mental note to return it, knowing full well she would probably forget until her dad would someday say, "Has anyone seen the super glue?"

They managed to piece the jar back together without any serious finger nicks or many glue smears on the glass. There was one little piece missing. Maybe the piece was two or more pieces, but there was only one hole, improbably shaped like a heart about the size of a quarter.

"So, now what?" Sam asked

"I don't know. You could put flowers in it, I guess. It just seems like you should keep it, since she went to all that trouble to bury it for you."

Sam studied her for a moment.

"What?" asked Hailey.

"You're completely buying this, aren't you?"

"Well, yeah. What other explanation is there?"

"Anybody could have buried the jar."

"So? That's not the point. She told us where it was."

"Someone told us," Sam said. "Anyway, someone wrote it in the diary. We don't know if it was a 'she.' It could still be Dad."

"How, how, how?"

"I don't know. I know it sounds impossible for Dad to have done it. He couldn't have done the video thing, probably, and he wasn't even around most of the time."

"And how do you explain the writing on the torn page? The one I stapled together."

"I don't know that, either! I keep going back and forth, believing, then not believing."

Sam rubbed her eyes with her fingertips, as if trying to clear them of cobwebs. She said, "I don't know how anyone else could have done any of this, but you're asking me to believe this is a ghost we're talking to."

"Writing to, actually."

"Yeah, like that's better."

Hailey said, "I don't think she's a ghost, exactly. I mean, she's probably dead all right. Now. She wasn't dead when she wrote this stuff, so she's not technically a ghost, right?"

The girls were quiet, contemplating the definition of ghost. Then, Sam said, "Should we tell Big?" Rachel was Big, as in big sister.

"Oh, hell no!" Hailey said.

"Why not?"

"Because she'd think we're total twerps."

"No she wouldn't. Would she?"

Hailey gave her a wide-eyed look and said, "Yes! She'd think we were pranking her." She looked away and added, "Besides, it's our deal. I'm not ready to let anyone else in on it. Not yet."

***

June 18, 2014, 2:15 pm

So, we found it. The jar. But, we didn't find the message. Anyways, we couldn't read the message. There were a couple of little scraps of paper that turned to dust when we touched them.

Oh, and hey, thanks for cutting my finger! The jar was broken, prob because of it being buried for years and the ground getting wet and freezing. I stuck my finger with one of the shards. No worries. I won't die, or anything.

Anyway, I'm not sure what this proves. I can't write the message back in the diary, because I couldn't read the message. I guess I can describe the jar. It has "Ball" written across the front of it, kind of slantwise and underlined. I have it here on my desk. We glued the pieces back together, all but one that is missing. Oh, and below "Ball" it says "Perfect Mason." Those words aren't underlined. The bottle is light blue and it has a gray cap. A gray ring, actually. It looks like the lid part rusted away.

This is so weird, because I'm trying to make you believe that we found the jar and so we're real. At the same time, I'm not totally sure I believe you are real.

I guess when—I just checked back for the date—June 28

rolls around, you'll believe in us for sure, because of that dead dude you'll read about in the papers.

The jar was a good idea. We were thinking it might be a really, really good idea if you could actually send something to us in the future that would still be perfect. Burying it doesn't work. Maybe you could hide it in some rocks.

And here's what we would like you to send us: Stamps! If your house is still the post office, maybe you could send a few stamps to us in a new jar. Make sure they have not been used. That is important. The jar needs to be sealed really good. Maybe you could melt wax all around the lid. What do you think?

If we get the stamps, we'll know you're real. And, if you don't tell us what the stamps look like, we can describe them to you and you'll know we're real. Deal? Kind of the "real deal!"

Your future friends, Sam and Hailey

"The 'real deal'?" Sam asked. "That is so lame."

"So, you write the next one."

Hailey shrugged. "You're the better writer, actually. I'm just messing with you."

Someone rapped twice on Sam's door and said, "I'm coming in. You'd better not be naked."

The girls turned to see Rachel open the door.

"What, we can't afford two chairs, now?"

Both girls looked down, as if it were the first time they'd noticed they were sharing a chair.

"Dweebs. You're gay for each other, aren't you?"

"What, no!" Sam said.

"We are so not!" added Hailey

"No need to get defensive. Be gay, if you want. I've got gay friends in college." Rachel nodded her head as if something had dawned on her. "Actually, it would be kind of cool to have a gay sister."

Nearly in unison, the girls said, "We're not gay!"

"Oh, that is so cute that you even say the same stuff together. In fact, that is. So. Very. Gay."

At that point Hailey and Sam sprung from their shared chair and tackled Rachel onto the bed. The three of them wrestled and shrieked on the covers for a minute until, by some unspoken agreement they stopped and just sprawled there, panting.

"Not gay," said Hailey.

"Whatever," Rachel said. Then she added, "Hey, you guys know I'm not a bigot or anything, right? I really wouldn't care if you were gay."

"But, we're..." Sam started.

"I know, I know. But, it really doesn't matter. Wouldn't matter, you know?"

In a serious voice, Hailey said, "Then maybe you should consider not using 'gay' like it was a bad word."

Rachel started to protest, then said, "Yeah, maybe. Sorry."

Sam said, "You should apologize to someone who is gay, not us."

"What?"

"Really, you should pick a random gay person and walk up to them and say, 'I'm sorry I'm such a jerk, but I'm such a jerk,'" Hailey said.

"I don't see that happening," Rachel said.

"I'd *like* to see it happen," said Sam.

"Okay, I'm a jerk and promise not to be jerky ever again."

Hailey said, "Not good enough."

"Best you're going to get, dweebs." Tired of the subject, Rachel changed it. "So, what have you two been doing since school got out."

Sam and Hailey gave each other a quick look.

"Nothing, really," Sam said.

Rachel said, "Come on, what was that look about. Boys? Somebody's got a boyfriend, right?"

"No, we don't have boyfriends," Sam said. "We really haven't been doing anything very exciting. Anyways, not as exciting as you. Tell us about the river trip."

Rachel was laughing and wrestling only a moment before. Now, her face changed. Something seemed to drop from in front of it leaving an empty face with a faraway look.

"You all right, Rach?" Sam asked.

"Yeah, I'm okay. I just... I'm not sure I want..." Rachel took in a long, slow breath. "I feel like I need to talk about it. Not to Mom and Dad, though. Not yet, anyway."

"Did something happen?" Hailey asked.

"Yes. Or, maybe it's something that didn't happen." Rachel's eyes squeezed shut and she sobbed. "I didn't die." Now, tears were rolling down her cheeks.

Sam got up and closed the door, then came back and sat on the bed next to her sister. She took one hand. Hailey wrapped her fingers around Rachel's other hand.

"Kleenex," Rachel sniffed.

Sam pulled three or four from the dispenser on her night table.

Rachel took them and started dabbing at her eyes and cheeks.

"I feel like a big baby," she said.

"No," Sam said. "Obviously, something bad happened."

Rachel nodded, took another breath, and began.

"I can't tell you how cool the trip was, at first. I mean, you've been on river floats where you splash each other and have water fights."

Both girls nodded.

"There was like none of that at all. You get on the river and you're blown away by the beauty. All the mountains and trees. We saw sheep. You know? Big horns? Lots of deer. Eagles and herons. We even saw a bear.

"So we're soaking in the wilderness—just jaw-dropping stuff—when the first rapids come up. Then there are more rapids and more rapids and more rapids. I mean, you really had to pay attention."

"You were paddling?" Hailey asked.

"Yeah, most of the time. There were three kinds of boats, so it all depended on which one you were in. If you were in a raft with a guide, they do all the paddling with those big long oars from the center of the boat. If you were in a paddle raft, you were sitting on the edge of the boat with, like, five others—three on each side. Everybody has a paddle, so everybody paddles. There's a river guide in the back who steers with a paddle once in a while, but mostly they just call out instructions to everyone, telling them where to go with the boat and how to get through the rapids."

"That sounds like a blast!" Hailey said. "Did they make you wear life jackets?"

"Oh, yeah. You do not get in a boat without a life jacket. They're serious about that. And, you have to wear a helmet, too, if you're in a kayak. Kind of like a bike helmet."

"So you don't hit your head on the rocks," Sam said. Rachel nodded.

"So, the other kind of boat is a kayak. They're not the hard ones that are made out of fiberglass or plastic. These are inflatables; two-person kayaks. Those were my favorite, at first."

"Did you crash one, or something?" Sam asked.

"Oh, yeah."

Hailey was about to make a smart remark, but she noticed how pale Rachel looked.

"I liked sitting in the back. That's where you can control things. You drag your paddle in the water if you want to turn, and the thing just spins so quick. And, they're faster than the rafts and more maneuverable. The fourth day out I was feeling like a pro. I was attacking those rapids. I couldn't wait to hit the whitewater.

"Well, I had a new partner in the front of the Kayak that morning, Katy."

"Katy your BFF?" Sam asked.

"Yeah, since third grade, and my sorority sister," Rachel's voice broke a little. "That Katy. We hadn't been in the kayak together until then. We were having fun, but I couldn't get her to pay attention to one thing they'd told us. They'd told us to keep way back from the rafts. I don't remember if they told us why, but it seemed like a good idea.

"Katy kept digging in with her paddle in front, like she was trying to catch up with the paddle boat ahead of us. I kept setting the paddle and pushing back to slow us down. Then this one time—the one time—we were only ten or fifteen feet behind the paddle boat as it went into this huge rapid. They got confused or something and ended up wrapping their boat."

"Wrapping it?" Hailey asked. "With what."

"Not wrapping it in something, wrapping around something. They got sideways in the river and hit a rock. The front of the raft tried to go around the rock on one side and the back tried to go around on the other. So they were stuck. Hung up on the rock. This all happened in, like, a second.

"Like I said, we were too close for me to steer us around it. We sort of slid in sideways right up against the raft. It wasn't even a hard hit, so I thought for a second we were fine. Then I felt the water suck us under. Next thing I knew I was beneath the paddle raft."

"In the water?" Hailey asked.

"Yeah, in the water. Under the water. I remember thinking that they had told us to walk out from under the raft with your hands if you were ever in that position. I was pretty calm about it, really, at that point. I felt the bottom of the raft with my fingers and started kind of pulling myself toward the edge. That's when the current caught me.

"I felt myself get sucked down into the river. Felt the rock go by on my right. I went down and down and down. It was like I was under the ocean. I looked up to the light and it seemed like it was 50 feet above me because it took me forever to swim to the surface. But really, it might have been 15 or 20 feet.

"That's when it came into my head that this might be it. This might really, really be the way I'd die."

Hailey and Sam stared at her. Rachel was breathing hard, like she was reliving the incident. When she began again, it was breathing she talked about.

"My lungs were on fire. I had swallowed water and I wanted so bad to cough, but I was still under water. Finally, my head popped above the surface. I was able to take a couple of breaths and cough, before I was swept into the next rapid. Later they told me they were about to cut the bottom out of the raft we'd hit because they thought I was trapped under there. The guide had her knife out and everything, when someone shouted that they could see my helmet in the water downstream."

"What about Katy?" Sam asked.

"They'd seen her pop up right away, then float away. The current pulled us both through another set of wild rapids. I was under the water more than I was on top. I kept bashing into rocks, so you won't see me wearing shorts for a while. My legs are a purple mess. But, at least I was able to get a breath every few seconds.

"Finally, one of the guides pulled the lead raft into an eddy ahead of me so they could fish me out as I floated by. I'll never forget that. I was so exhausted and out of breath. It felt like someone had shoved a fire hose up my nose. I saw someone reaching for me from the raft. I wanted to grab, but I couldn't quite reach it. This guy—I don't even know who it was—stretched out farther and I stretched out farther. Finally, just the tips of our fingers touched. It was like that Michelangelo painting, you know, where God has his finger out to Adam? I mean, we were touching fingertips and somehow—I guess it was adrenaline or something—I lunged for it. Then he could hook one of his fingers around one of mine, and that was enough. He pulled and grabbed my hand. When I got near the raft someone grabbed the straps of my life preserver and they pulled me in.

"Wow," said Sam.

"Yeah, wow. It was like the best moment of my life. I just sprawled across the raft on everybody's legs. There was something in the bottom of the raft and it was sticking me in the ribs and really hurt but I didn't care. I could breath!"

"Oh, Big, no wonder you're upset," Sam said.

"Yeah, but no. That wasn't the end of it. I was fine, but they hadn't found Katy. Everybody on all the rafts was frantic looking for her. It must have only been maybe a minute after they pulled me out that they found her. She was floating in a little hole on the back side of a big rock. She was unconscious."

And, here Rachel broke down in sobs.

"She wasn't even *breathing!*"

Hailey's hands went to her cheeks as her mouth gaped open.

"They got her out fast and got her to a sandbar. Two of the guides got her out of her life jacket and they started doing CPR. By this time I was on the sandbar, too, but they wouldn't let me near her."

Sam grabbed the box of tissues and shoved them at her sister.

"Thanks." Rachel wiped her eyes, blew her nose, and went on. "It seemed forever. Then, she coughed and started spitting up water. I mean, she was blue and everything. But she started to breathe. Then, they let me get next to her and all I could do was tell her how sorry I was."

Hailey said, "But it wasn't your fault."

"Maybe. Maybe not. There might have been something I could have done to avoid the raft, if I knew what I was doing. Anyway, I was sorry, but at the same time I was so flippin' happy that she was alive. I mean, I didn't even notice that I was practically naked."

"What?" Hailey asked.

"I'd lost my top. I was kayaking in shorts and a bikini top. The river stripped that off somewhere along the way. One of the other girls put a shirt over my shoulders and I finally got a clue." Rachel laughed at that through her tears.

Sam threw her arms around Rachel's neck. Hailey did the same and they all three collapsed back on the bed. They laughed the laughter of release, the kind that comes at the end of great peril. Rachel gave first Sam, then Hailey kisses on their foreheads.

"Who's gay, now?" Hailey said. "You're kissing *girls*!"

***

It was nearly 10 p.m. when Sam's mom kicked Hailey out. The three girls had spent hours together, mostly listening to Rachel's stories about college life.

Sam was exhausted. It did not occur to her to even peek at the diary before going to bed. The next morning, it was the first thing on her mind. She opened it to discover another entry.

JUNE 2014

Sunday	Monday	Tuesday	Wednesday	Thursday	Friday	Saturday
	2	3	4	5	6	7
8	9	10	11	12	13	14
15 B Day!	16	17	18	19	20	21
22	23	24	25	26	27	28 Duke Dies
29	30					

June 19, 1914

I cannot believe you went to the trouble to describe a jar! Everyone knows what they look like! That is no kind of proof!

I know, a bottle that was buried for a hundred years might be broken. I should have considered that. Those rings are coated with zinc, of course, so should not rust. Why would the lid rust?

Paper would not last that long if it got wet, which it would in a broken jar.

Now you want stamps? No, our house is no longer the post office. It's intriguing that you would know that it once was. I think no one would know it in a hundred years. Most people my age would not know it now. I do, because I live here. So that makes me think I am dealing with an adult. You want stamps? Is this an elaborate scheme to have me give you some free stamps!?

Stamps would not survive a broken bottle. I think I know how to solve that. I will do some looking & measuring, first.

I have to say that, whomever you are, you spend little time on your spelling. Earlier you mentioned a Duke who would be killed. This time you said "dead dude." Which is it, a dude or a Duke?

Sam slammed the diary shut. It seemed like no matter what they did, nothing proved anything. She stuffed the diary under her bed on the theory that hiding it in different places would confuse... whoever. Whomever? Who used 'whomever'? Whatever. She had to pee.

Never one to waste an idle moment without texting Hailey, Sam texted:

Another 1. Frustrating. No prrof.

She didn't usually correct texting errors, but that comment about the duke dude nagged at her. She started to delete the last word. That's when it happened.

One minute she was holding her ancient phone and the next minute she heard a little plop.

She got up, pulled her PJ bottoms up, and stared into the toilet. She could barely see the end of her phone at the bottom of the basin.

"Oh, shit, shit, shit!" Sam shook her hands as she said it, as if they were already wet. And yucky.

She looked around to see if there was anything she could fish it out with. She spotted her toothbrush. Way too short. Waaaaay too icky. She opened the cabinet under the sink and found a toilet brush.

Sam didn't much like touching the handle. She did so using as few fingers as possible. Maneuvering the brush without really touching it—it occurred to her she should have wrapped TP around the handle—was tricky. She was able to touch the phone with the end of the brush. Pushing past the phone, she tried to hook the brush around behind it. When she thought she had it, she jerked back, hoping the phone would come all the way out. No chance. The move did cause the phone to fly up out of the bottom of the toilet, take a waterslide ride around the rim, and dive back down the hole. Clear down the hole.

"Oh no! Damn it!"

Sam probed with the brush. Maybe she could feel the phone. Maybe she was pushing it further down. Either way, it had disappeared from sight.

She sat on the floor and thought. She was so screwed. The phone had to be ruined by now. If she could get it out, she'd try putting it in a container of rice. She'd heard that dried them out, sometimes. She'd Google it. There must be something that would work. Surely they had come up with something since the last two times she'd gotten a phone wet.

Wait. She could say she lost it. That would be better than getting it wet, again. She'd never lost one. That was a point in her favor, right? So, the thing to do was to flush the toilet and make sure it worked. If it worked okay, she could make up a story about how it must have fallen out of her backpack on the ride. She could even go look for it.

In her head, the math added up to trying the toilet. So, Sam stood up and pressed the lever. Instead of seeing the water circle the toilet then disappear, the bowl started filling. It filled all the way to the rim and started cascading over in a near perfect circle of falling water. Under other circumstances one could even call the display tranquil.

"Daaaaaad!"

***

Sam spent the rest of the morning apologizing, cleaning the bathroom, apologizing, and begging for a new phone.

"You must be *kidding*!" her dad said. "You have the nerve to ask for a new phone after ruining your *third* one?"

"It was an accident."

"An accident that wouldn't have happened if you'd just left it in your room instead of taking your phone to the bathroom," her mother said. "You really can't get along without it long enough to pee?"

"I know. I should have been more careful. I promise. I really, really promise I'll be more careful with a new one."

Rachel said, "So, this was, like, your new iPhone?"

"No, it was my old crappy phone."

"But, you've still got the iPhone?"

"She didn't have an iPhone," her mother said.

"But, I thought she was getting one for her birthday."

Their mother glared at Sam.

"What?" Sam said. "I only told Rach I thought I was getting one."

"So, what did you get?" Rachel asked.

"That really isn't the point of the conversation, now, is it?" their father asked.

"I got her some summer shorts and Chris got her a diary," said Mrs. Reed.

"Whoa, you missed that prediction by a mile, Dweeb,"

Rachel said.

Sam said, "It was all really great." She heard the lack of enthusiasm in her own voice. It brightened when she said, "But this does give us the chance to save a little money."

Her dad gave her a skeptical look.

"I noticed that there's a new iPhone upgrade out. Not a whole new phone, but some new features. That means the older one, the one I wanted, is a hundred dollars cheaper." Without taking a breath she continued. "And so, if you had gotten me one for my birthday it would have been a hundred dollars more, but you didn't, and now it's a hundred dollars less, so this is really an opportunity to save money." She saw by her dad's face that he wasn't buying it. "A hundred dollars," she concluded, in a much diminished voice.

"Saving money is an excellent idea," her dad said. "Why don't you start right now. As soon as you get $500 together, you'll be able to buy that new phone."

"Me? Save what? I barely get an allowance, and there aren't any jobs."

Her dad shrugged. "It will take a few months..."

"Months!? Dad, I can't get along without a phone for months, or even weeks."

"Oh, I think you'll find that you can."

"How would I communicate? How would I talk to Hailey?"

Her mother said, "Well, first, you could talk to her. We still have a land line."

Yes, like they were living in the 70s, her parents had

a land line. She couldn't remember the last time she had called out with it. She rarely even picked it up when it rang, knowing that none of her friends would ever call her number at home.

"You still have the computer," her mother said. "You can email Hailey."

"Email? Wow, Mom, do people even do that?" Rachel asked.

"Butt out, Big," her mom said. Even her parents called Rachel Big, sometimes. They hadn't yet taken to calling Sam Dweeb.

"Sammy, you're right about one thing," their dad said. "This is an opportunity. It's an opportunity for you to earn your next phone. It's an opportunity for you to learn to be more careful with your possessions."

"How am I going to earn it? I'm barely 14. Nobody's going to hire me."

"I'll hire you," said her dad. "You can help me at the Big House. There's a lot of cleaning and sanding to be done. I bet your mom can find things for you to do around here where you could earn a little extra money."

"Like what, clean my room?"

"No," her mom said. "You don't get paid for cleaning your room. The basement, maybe, and the garage. I've got a ton of weeding I could..."

"Weeding!? I hate, weeding!"

"I don't like it either," said her mom. "And you don't have to do it, if you don't want to. But, then, I don't have to pay you, either."

Rachel said, "Maybe you could clean my room." She glanced at her mother. "Would that count?"

"Not with me, but you can pay her, if you like."

The phone rang. Chris Reed picked it up.

"Reed residence." He looked over at Sam while listening to the response, then said, "No, Hailey, she hasn't had a stroke. She's right here." He handed the receiver to Sam.

"'Lo."

"WTF," Hailey said. It didn't work as well in speech as it did in text.

"I dropped my phone in the toilet."

"Oh, my god! I thought you'd had..."

"A stroke, I know. It's ruined, so I won't be texting for a while."

"Hey, this is a chance to get a new iPhone."

"I wish. That's what I've been telling my folks." Sam turned away from everyone in the room and cupped her hand around the mouthpiece. "They aren't buying it."

"They aren't buying you a phone?"

"No, I mean... No, they aren't buying the argument. Or the phone. They're making me work for it."

"That's so unfair!"

"Tell me about it."

"Can I come over? Are they, like, still beating on you, or anything?"

Sam turned back around. "Can she come over?"

Her mom shrugged. "Sure. Maybe she can help pull weeds."

Sam sent her the best anti-weeding look she could muster.

"Come on over."

***

They spent the first 15 minutes in Sam's room commiserating about how mean and unfair her parents were. Then, Sam let Hailey read the latest diary entry.

"I can't believe she doesn't believe us," Hailey said.

"I know, right? What's it going to take?"

"I mean, we believe her."

"We do?"

"Don't we? I kinda think the whole buried jar thing is a pretty big coincidence."

Sam wasn't sure what to say. A part of her wanted to believe. Another part was afraid her dad, or someone else, would jump out from behind a door and yell "Gotcha!" She despised being the butt of someone's joke.

But now, as the writing started crawling across the page, working its way beneath Hailey's thumb and out the other side toward the far edge of the paper, Sam finally and at last believed.

She gasped and slapped her hand to her mouth.

"What?"

With her free hand, Sam pointed a trembling finger at the diary.

Hailey looked down, stared at what was happening for about two seconds, then dropped the diary to the floor.

"Ohmygod, ohmygod!" Hailey said.

They both looked at the diary now laying face down, its

pages rumpled.

Hailey grabbed a pen, then picked up the diary.

"You're going to *touch* it?" Sam asked.

Hailey flipped to the page where the writing had appeared. It was still going. With shaking hands she put the pen to paper just ahead of where the writing was headed and wrote *"Stop!"*

The writing stopped. To this point it had said,

June 19, 1914

Another jar it is, then. It makes me angry with myself to give the benefit of the doubt to a prankster. One last time I will play along! I put stamps in this jar, so you can describe those for me. I closed it with a zinc lid & sealed it with candle wax. Then I hid it in

That was where Hailey had written *"Stop!"* The writing had stopped. The girls stared at the page, waiting for something to happen. When nothing did, Hailey said, "Did I break it?"

"No. I don't think so. How are you feeling right now?"

"Scared as shit."

"Me, too. My hands won't stop shaking. Maybe she's scared, too."

"Why would she be scared? She's the freaking ghost!"

"No, she's not. Remember? If this is real, she's a girl. She's alive in her time, even if she isn't alive now."

"That doesn't make any sense."

"If you believe this is happening, it does. I mean, we've totally eliminated Dad, haven't we?"

"Totally."

"Then, this is a girl who is just as scared as we are. If she saw you write 'stop,' she's probably barricaded in her bathroom now with the diary laying on the floor on the other side of the door. She's got to be out of her mind with fear. She already thinks we might be the devil."

"Maybe she's the devil."

Sam didn't have an answer for that.

"Gimme the pen," Sam said. She took it from Hailey along with the diary and began writing.

Sorry to scare you. But, you scared us! We saw your writing appear on the page like a ghost was doing it. So, we—Hailey—thought maybe you could see it if we wrote in the diary at the very same time. I think that worked. So, like I said, sorry to scare you.

One good thing. We believe you! I bet you believe us, now, too!

Please finish telling us where you put the new jar. We already believe you, but it is important that we have the stamps for another reason.

Your Friend,

Sam

When Hailey finished reading it, she asked, "Why is it important about the stamps?"

"Because I need a new iPhone," Sam said.

JUNE 2014

Sunday	Monday	Tuesday	Wednesday	Thursday	Friday	Saturday
1	2	3	4	5	6	7
8	9	10	11	12	13	14
15 *B Day!*	16	17	18	19	20	21
22	23	24	25	26	27	28 *Duke Dies*
29	30					

The next morning Sam called Hailey on the land line.

"She finally answered."

"Cool! I thought we'd scared her to death."

"Practically did. At least she believes us, now."

"And we believe her?" Hailey asked.

"Well, duh."

Hailey said, "I guess it's pretty certain. What did she say?"

"Like I'm going to tell you that over the phone?"

"Oh, yeah. I'll be right over."

After they had passed through Sam's room, made the little leap to the branch and crawled into the Library, Sam handed the diary to Hailey.

June 20, 1914

Please do not write while I am writing. Please. I have never had such a scare! I imagined the diary was on fire in my hands. I threw it to the floor & ran from the room. I did not go back in for hours.

When I "screwed my courage to the sticking place" I found the pages were not burnt, as I thought they might be. Even so, my hands trembled when I picked it up. A part of me wanted to throw it away or truly burn it. But I saw your writing & decided to at least read it. Is that how the devil works? Does he entice you just enough to bring you along an inch at a time?

This seems devilish in many ways. Yet, you do not. You Sam & you Hailey seem like girls. I have gone back and read this from the start. You use words I don't understand & your way of talking—your way of writing, is strange. You seem to think the same of me. How could it be otherwise if we are truly a hundred years apart?

I know only that this is really happening to me. I think it is happening to you. If this is not the doings of the Devil, then what? Is it the work of God? Why would He bother with someone like me? Why would the Devil?

I spent a night without sleep thinking of this. A hundred times I vowed to stop. A hundred times I decided to continue, to see what would happen. A hundred and one, the latter.

So, for now, I will continue.

I'm sorry you were frightened by my writing. I know that feeling well. Let us agree to scare each other as little as possible.

With my resolve to write comes a new way of thinking about the world. I must now imagine how my actions will change it. If you found the bottle I buried, I changed the world for you. It was in a very small way, but it changed. If I send another bottle into the future, more surely than a note in a bottle thrown into the waves of the ocean, what changes will come of it? I see no harm in stamps, though I wonder why you want them. Every home must have a telephone in the future. Mr. Bell has already made a coast-to-coast call. Why would you need letters? More to my point, why would you need stamps?

I have resolved to play along, so you will have your stamps. You have them now, though you do not know it. I have hidden the jar in the ice cave. It is five feet in. I measured it. You will find it on the left about halfway up the wall. There is a little hole there of a size that makes one think it was made exactly for this. God, or the Devil again, perhaps. I placed the jar in the hole & put a rock from the floor of the cave in front of it.

Let me know when you find it, future friends. Oh, I hope that last is true and that you are not the worst kind of trouble!!!

"I wonder if we are," Hailey said, when she finished reading the entry.

"Are what?"

"The worst kind of trouble. Can we get her in trouble doing this?"

"I don't see how," Sam said. "You don't mean because of that devil stuff, do you?"

Hailey was slow to answer. "No. Not exactly. You know I don't believe all that religious stuff. Not really. My units do. Sometimes—not often—they're right about some things."

"So, you think they might be right about the devil?"

"No, of course not. Not really, anyway. I mean, there's a chance, I suppose."

"This is something else," Sam said. "It feels more like magic, like Harry Potter."

"Do you believe in Harry Potter?"

"No, of course not. He's just a character. There might be things we don't understand. They might seem like magic because we don't understand them. Like, what if Emma suddenly saw a TV. Wouldn't she think that was magic?"

Hailey frowned. "Maybe. She sees movies. She'd probably think it was like a smaller movie."

"Okay, bad example. Ummm, microwaves. What if she saw us use a microwave? Her family cooks on that big, stupid iron stove. She probably has to chop wood for it and stuff."

"Yeah, a microwave would be magic. So would a computer. At least she knows about telephones."

"Wasn't that funny?" Sam asked. "She thinks we use telephones instead of writing letters."

"Well, we do. We text, right?"

"Yeah, but that's not what she expected. She thought we'd all talk to each other with the telephone and that nobody would write letters."

"That's actually a pretty awesome prediction," Hailey said.

"Sure, but people still write letters. Dad still pays bills and uses stamps."

"Still awesome. I wouldn't have a clue how things might be in a hundred years. We might be living on Mars. Would we still have phones? Would people call their friends on Mars? Would we cook with lasers or something?"

Without waiting for an answer Hailey got up and started out of the tree house.

"Where you going?"

"Computer. There's stuff I need to know."

Sam followed her back into the bedroom. Hailey cranked up the computer and started rattling the keys. In less than a minute, she said, "You're right," as if conceding a point.

"Of course I am. About what?"

"The wooden stove."

"You mean the wood-burning stove?"

"Whatever. I thought maybe Emma used that red electric stove. It says here that electric stoves didn't really catch on until the 1930s, because so many places didn't even have electricity."

"I told you, that stove is from the 1950s," Sam said. "Emma would still be chopping wood."

"That sounds sucky."

"No kidding."

After a moment considering the sucky-ness of chopping wood, Hailey said, "So, let's go get the stamps."

Sam broke into a grin. "You know where the ice cave is?"

"Me? No. I thought you'd know?"

"Why would I know?"

"Because... because she's your grandmother. I thought maybe your dad might have said something."

"Wait, what? She's not my grandmother. Her name was Agnes. Or, no, that was my great-grandmother, I think."

"Well, she has to be something. Some kind of relative. You have the same name and she lived in the Big House."

"I guess," Sam said.

"I'll get my mother working on it."

"On what?"

"On your genealogy. We'll make a Mormon out of you yet!"

***

That evening, Sam tried to find out about the ice cave.

"Dad, is there an ice cave around here somewhere? Maybe somewhere by the Big House."

Chris Reed looked up from his plate and said, "An ice cave? Where did you hear about that?"

Sam shrugged, "I don't know. Somebody mentioned it once. I was just wondering."

"Well, I've wondered about that for years. Grandma used to talk about it, some. They would use the ice from the cave for their icebox. She said people were jealous because it was so close. Others used it, too, but they had to go further to get the ice. I was too little to think about asking her about where it was. She died before it occurred to me, and Mom didn't know where it was."

"What was her name, again?" Sam asked.

"Grandma? Agnes."

"That's what I was thinking, that my grandma's name was Agnes."

"No, *my* grandma's name was Agnes. She was your great-grandmother. *Your* grandmother was my mother. Her name was Maxine."

"It's confusing."

"I suppose," her dad said.

"So, you don't know where the ice cave is?"

"I don't. I looked for it years ago, but didn't have any luck."

"Could it just go away?"

"I don't see how," he said. "Well, maybe. I suppose the ceiling might have caved in. More likely brush grew up around it when people quit using it."

"So, it could still be there?"

"Sure. It probably is, if we knew where to look. Do you want to look for it?"

She did. She did not want her dad's help.

"Nah. I was just curious."

She thought she saw her dad's shoulders slump a little when she said that, which made her feel a little guilty.

***

That evening, she wrote:

June 20, 2014

One problem: I don't know where the ice cave is. Neither does my dad, though he had heard of it. We don't use a lot of ice anymore.

JUNE 2014

Sunday	Monday	Tuesday	Wednesday	Thursday	Friday	Saturday
1	2	3	4	5	6	7
8	9	10	11	12	13	14
15 B Day!	16	17	18	19	20	21
22	23	24	25	26	27	28 Duke Dies
29	30					

When Sam woke in the morning, she reached beneath her mattress and pulled out the diary. She was not surprised to see that Emma had made another entry.

June 21, 1914

How do you not use ice? Is it cold where you live, year around? But no, you live where I live. Weather hasn't changed, surely.

I have always thought I lived in modern times. There are so many new inventions. You truly live there! In modern times, I mean. So, you must have a way to keep food cool in spite of the heat of the day.

But, losing the ice cave is hard to credit. It has been so important to us ever since grandfather homesteaded here.

I think the cave is not lost. If you no longer have need for ice, people probably forgot where it was. It must still be there. How to guide you to it? It is among the rocks on the north side of the upper valley. There is quite a lot of brush there, everywhere but the cave entrance. If people quit going there, I suppose the brush would fill in. So, all you need to do is cut away some brush to find it. I wish I could leave you a sign that said, "Look here, Sam!" I would have difficulty explaining that, & the sign would not last a hundred years. A pile of rocks might work. I could make a pyramid, like the Egyptians!

If I can move the rocks, so can someone else, so that might not work. We need something that will last a hundred years & that someone else won't move.

I have it! I will plant a tree! Cottonwood cuttings would do well there, because of the ditch. Did I mention the ditch? No, I see. There is a ditch that follows along the base of the bluff. This very day I will go make a cutting and plant it along the ditch bank near the entrance to the cave. You will know where to cut away the brush that must now cover it.

But, what if someone cuts down the tree? I can't think of that. I must try it. If it works, you will have a tree to mark the spot. If it doesn't, you can tell me tomorrow & I will try something else.

That is the most remarkable thing. I can plant a tree today & tomorrow you can tell me if it is still growing in one hundred years. It makes me swoon to think of it! You must go as soon as possible and tell me if my tree is there! First, I must plant it, of course. But If I do plant it—did plant it?—the tree is there now in your time.

Find the tree. Find the cave. Find the jar! Oh, and tell me why you need stamps.

***

Sam rode her bike to Hailey's. From there, they biked

together to the valley of the Big House. She hadn't really thought of it as a valley until Emma mentioned it. There was a river there, with low mountains on one side and an even lower hill on the other. So, yes, it was a valley. She just hadn't noticed. What else had she missed? Where trees grew, for one thing. What direction was north, for another. Hailey could help with that once they got there.

They pumped along at a good pace for the first three miles, seeing not a single car. Then, a beat up old Mustang convertible came their way.

Three boys rode in the yellow and primer-colored car with the top down. They passed by the girls going fast. The squeal of brakes caused the girls to look back over their shoulders.

"Oh, crap! That's Jacob in back!"

"You know them?"

"Sort of. Jacob goes to my church."

"*You* don't even go to your church, Hailey."

"Sometimes the units make me," she said. "Besides, he's been going there since forever."

The car started backing toward them.

"What do we do?" Hailey half-whispered.

"Are they dangerous?"

"No! They're hot!"

Why that meant the girls had to "do" something, Sam couldn't guess.

"Hey, it is you," one of the boys said. He was the one sitting in back.

Hailey and Sam stopped and each put down a foot.

"Hey, Jacob," Hailey said.

"Hey, yourself. I almost didn't recognize you. There's something different."

Hailey blushed. Big. It was like she had a sudden sunburn.

"Who's your friend?" Jacob asked.

Hailey looked too flustered to answer.

"Sam Reed," Sam said. "Nice to meet you."

"Yeah, same."

"Jake, I thought these were chicks you knew," said the driver.

"I know them. Anyway, I know Hailey."

"They're little girls. We'll probably get arrested just for talking to them."

At that, Hailey said, "We are not little girls. We're 14." In fact, Hailey wouldn't be 14 for a couple of weeks.

"Oh, my mistake." The driver laughed. "You're practically in college!"

"C'mon, let's get outta here," said the boy riding shotgun.

The driver revved the engine, said, "Goodbye girls," and popped the clutch.

The rear tires chirped and they were off, again. From the back seat, Jake called "I've got it! No makeup, right?"

The tires chirped every time the driver hit another gear.

"Shit, shit, shit!" Hailey said, a triple expletive that would make her mother, whose strongest expression was "word," faint.

"What?" Sam asked.

"I can't believe we ran into him when I wasn't wearing makeup. I look like a baby!"

"You look fine."

"Yeah, right! That's why they called me a little girl!"

"They're dorks. Why do you care? Besides, they called me a little girl, too. Screw them."

"They're *seniors*," Hailey said, as if that explained everything. "They're laughing at us right now!"

For the next three miles Sam tried to cheer up her friend. Hailey got quieter and quieter. By the time they reached the gravel road, Hailey had even quit grunting in response.

From the gravel road, which followed along below the ridge of the hill, you couldn't really see much of the river, just a flash of water now and then. The willows along its banks marked its meander through the valley. There were big squares of crops planted on most of the land on both sides of the river. Sam didn't know what kind of crops. Hay, she thought. Maybe wheat. Potatoes?

Her grandparents had farmed. Some of her cousins, who she hardly knew, were farmers. They still lived in the valley. Those were their crops and their cattle she could see as brown and white blobs in the distance.

For as much as her dad cared about the Big House that sat right in the middle of all these fields, he didn't have much interest in farming. He had inherited some of the land in the valley, including the house, but she thought he'd sold it to one of the cousins. Or maybe they rented it from him.

Now that she thought about it, who owned the land where the cave was? Would they be trespassing? Maybe someone would shoot at them to scare them off. Nah, that sounded crazy. They were her cousins. They would know her. Wouldn't they?

As they rode past the Big House, Hailey asked, "So, do you know where we're going to find this tree?"

"She said at the upper end of the valley on the north side. Which side is that?"

"We're on the north side."

"Good. We won't have to cross the river." A thought came to Sam. "Maybe we passed it. Were there trees on the other end of the valley?"

"She said upper valley, didn't she?"

"I think so."

Hailey nodded up the road. "That's the upper end."

"How do you know?"

"It's where the river comes from. It flows back toward town, so that's the upper end."

Sam wasn't absolutely certain she got that. Hailey was the one who understood directions. That was good enough.

Had Sam previously been on the road where it went past the Big House? Maybe. She couldn't remember when. She noticed a big row of trees along a fence line below them. Something made the ground look different on this side of the trees. Maybe an old road? Or, an old ditch? The grass was a little taller and darker there.

The trees were not in good shape. Stark, white branches dominated, sticking straight into the sky. Little patches of leaves clung to the sides of some of the branches. Were these cottonwoods? Emma had said she would plant one tree, not a whole row of them.

The hillside they were riding on dropped away to form a low cliff on their right as they went. Lava rocks stuck up at the end of the green field. They made it look dry and dead there. A sprinkler on wheels tick, tick, ticked away between the road and the little cliff. Rainbows shimmered through the spray of water.

Hailey, who knew directions, rode a little ways in front. She coasted down a hill, then stood to pedal up the other side. Sam did the same. When they got to the top of the hill they saw that the road turned to the left and disappeared over the through the fields. But the valley continued on ahead of them. A short dirt road dropped off at the curve and ran between some outbuildings and a tidy little house.

Hailey stopped. "What do you think?" she asked, when Sam pulled beside her.

"She said at the upper end of the valley. She didn't mention a road."

"She didn't say anything about a house, either."

"Probably wasn't even built back then," said Sam.

They could see that the house and sheds were nestled into a little curve of the hill, which continued on beyond the buildings. The valley narrowed a mile or so beyond the farmhouse. They could see taller cliffs ahead forming a canyon where the river tumbled out of the mountains.

"There are some trees here," Hailey said.

"Yeah, in someone's yard."

Hailey said, "There are more rocks along the edge of the hill beyond the buildings. Didn't she talk about rocks?"

"She said the cave was in a cliff and that she might pile up rocks like a pyramid."

"Well, there's more cliff just across there. Can't see a tree, though."

"We should ride through," Sam said.

"Do you know these people?" Hailey asked.

"Maybe. They're probably cousins."

"Shouldn't we ask permission?"

Before Sam could answer, she heard a screen door slam. A middle-aged woman wearing a headscarf came off the porch and started to move a lawn sprinkler.

Sam made her pedals turn and coasted down the dirt road, stopping in front of the gate to the woman's house. It was a picket gate in a picket fence that was gray with chips and strips of white paint curling in places.

The woman looked up as Sam skidded to a stop.

"Well, hello," she said. "I didn't even see you."

"Hi," Sam said.

"Hi," said Hailey. They both used small voices.

"What brings you girls riding way out here," asked the woman. She walked toward them drying her hands on her jeans.

"We're sort of exploring," Sam said.

"Yeah, we're looking for a cave," said Hailey.

Sam wanted to kill her.

"Or anything. We're just looking at rocks."

"A cave?" the woman asked. "I don't think there's a cave

around here. You girls don't want to be messing around in a cave, anyway, do you?"

"Well,..."

"You're Sammy, aren't you? Chris and Amanda's daughter?"

"Yes, Ma'am," Sam said.

"And, who's your friend?"

"I'm Hailey. Hailey Poulsen."

"O'Dell and Noreen's girl?"

"One of them," Hailey said. "The good one."

The woman laughed. "You've got some brothers and sisters, don't you?"

"A few," Hailey said. She smiled a smile that looked recently purchased.

"What's this about a cave?" the woman asked.

"Well, not necessarily a cave," said Sam, trying to save the secret. "We just want to explore the rocks."

"Yeah," said Hailey. "The rocks above your place, if you wouldn't mind."

"Up there? You mean the Indian writing?"

Sam knew nothing about Indians and what they might write about, but it sounded like a good diversion to her.

"Yeah, that."

"Well, we get people out here once in a while to look at that. Your dad tell you about it?"

Sam nodded.

"You're more than welcome to take a look. Do you know where it is? No, of course you don't," the woman said. "I have bread in the oven or I'd show you. But you really can't get very lost. Bike on down there on the other side of that shed." She pointed. "Follow the road down along the fence for about a quarter mile. You'll see the cliff on your left. Walk up to the cliff and you'll see the writing if you look long enough. Mind the snakes."

"Snakes?" Hailey asked.

"Rattlesnakes. Careful where you step. Don't turn over any rocks. If you don't step right on one, the snakes won't hurt you. They'll make that buzzing sound to warn you off. You hear that, just slowly step away." She waved one hand as if shooing off a pesky mosquito. "You'll be fine. We hardly ever see any."

Hailey followed Sam around the shed the woman had pointed to and along the narrow, dusty dirt road.

"Snakes!?" Hailey said, through clenched teeth.

"She said they wouldn't bother us."

"Well, they bother *me!*"

"We'll be careful."

"They give me the creeps!"

Snakes did not bother Sam, much. Now, spiders, that was another story. She hated spiders passionately. Whenever she found one in the bathroom she and Rachel shared, she would scream until Big came to her rescue with a shoe or more likely a drinking glass. Rach was always capturing spiders in drinking glasses and tossing them out the window with the advice, "Go play."

Because of spiders, Sam did not make fun of Hailey's aversion to snakes. What scared you, scared you. Simple as that. She respected Hailey's fear, but not enough to turn around and forget about the cave, just enough so that she didn't make fun of her.

"We'll be really, really careful," Sam said. "Let's just find the tree."

They rode parallel with the low cliff, about 50 feet from its face, at the foot of the sloping hill below it. Sam thought she could make out what had once been an irrigation ditch right at the foot of the cliff. There were piles of dirt that didn't look natural.

"Lots of brush," Hailey said.

"No tree, though."

They rode back and forth along the cliff, searching for a tree. On the third pass, Hailey said, "Wait. Isn't that, like, a log?"

Sam stopped and looked where she pointed. Something grayish white lay pointed down the slope toward them.

"Let's go see."

Sam was off her bike and making her way through the sagebrush and cheat grass when Hailey yelled, "Be careful!"

This was a switch. Of the two, Hailey was always the more adventurous. She rarely held back.

"Yeah, yeah," Sam said. Nevertheless, she did start watching where she put her feet.

It was a log. The strangest one Sam had ever seen. It was broken into two major pieces, with splinters of dry, rotting wood scattered all around. She tested it with her foot. The log was much lighter than expected. Sam rolled it toward her and found it was completely hollow. A big split ran down the length of the largest piece. She pushed against each edge of the split and the entire log burst apart.

"Wow! This thing doesn't weigh ten pounds!"

"Fascinating," Hailey called from the road, pretending to yawn.

"I bet this is it. It was a tree, once. I can see a little of the stump and roots."

Sam found the remains of the ditch. It was grown over, mostly with cheat grass. Her socks were already full of the pointy little seeds. There was no sign of water, only a shallow trench where once it ran. From bank to bank the abandoned ditch was about six feet wide. On the far side, a tangle of brush blocked access to the cliff.

"Come on up," Sam called. "Help me look."

Hailey grumbled, but started picking her way through the grass and up the hill.

Meanwhile, Sam slipped a tiny flashlight out of her pack. She got down on her knees and pointed the light into the base of the bushes. Down near the ground there weren't as many branches. She could see a couple of holes in the bushes that might let her slither under and back to the base of the cliff behind.

Slither. Thinking that word almost made her shudder. Snakes weren't her special fear, but the thought of one slithering up the leg of her jeans was a little creepy.

"You're not getting me in there!"

The sound of Hailey's voice right behind her gave Sam resolve.

"Fine. You stay here and watch for snakes."

Sam slid her backpack off and got down on her hands and knees. She moved bigger branches out of her way and snapped smaller ones off. A few inches at a time she entered the gloom beneath the bushes. Branches scraped at her arms and snagged her shirt when they weren't poking her in the ribs.

It took her a couple of minutes to work her way through to the other side of the brush. She stood. There was barely room to stand. The cliff was right there. Lichen-covered slabs of black rock with cracks and crevices rose above her.

Black was an easy description of the color of the rock, but it fell short of the reality. It was really mottled from red to brown to jet, with shadows knitting it all together. Sam stood so close to the cliff her eyes wouldn't focus for a moment. When they did, she saw a stick figure on the rock right in front of her. It looked like it was once red, but time and the elements had worked away the color until it was a dull brown against the darker rock.

It was like no stick figure she had seen. It had an extra long body, for one thing, and no head. Just a neck. It's arms were held out straight on either side, with the forearms bent down at the elbows. Even weirder, the legs were the same way, almost as if the figure were squatting.

As Sam studied the drawing, she saw another above it and another to one side. They were drawn the same way, only smaller. Then she spotted something else. It looked like someone had drawn two little mountains, one in front of the other, with what looked like a beard below them.

And there. There was something like a sun.

"I found the Indian writing," Sam called to Hailey.

"Cool. What do they have to say?"

"Don't know. It's not really writing. It's, like, pictures."

"Petroglyphs?"

"Yeah, I guess they are. Yeah, I've seen them in books before, but never the real thing. It is kind of cool. Come look."

"Pass," Hailey said.

"I already scared away all the snakes."

"That's what they'd like you to think."

Sam continued to look for more petroglyphs. She found one that looked like it might be a dog. There was another set of men—people, anyway. These were carrying bows. Maybe.

As she moved along the cliff face looking for more, she came to a huge slab of lava that had broken away to form a big, squarish boulder one side of which stood away about six feet from the cliff. There was bare dirt around it and leading into the darkness behind. There was a trace of animal tracks in the dirt. Sam could not guess what kind of animal had made them. She clicked on her flashlight and pointed it behind the boulder.

"Oh my god! Hailey, I've found it! This is the cave! It has to be!"

"Really?"

"Yes. At least, I think so. You've got to come see this!"

Hailey made some more noises about snakes, but Sam wasn't paying attention. She followed the beam of her light into the cavern. She saw a glint of ice far back in the cave, maybe 40 feet. Sam wasn't good at distances. That's why she'd stuck a measuring tape she'd borrowed from her mother's sewing basket into the pocket of her jeans.

Five feet wasn't far. She'd barely have to enter the cave at all. But where had Emma measured from? The mouth of the cave, of course, but where was that, exactly? Was it where she stepped behind the big rock? It was almost like a part of the cave. For a moment she wondered if it had fallen down, somehow, and blocked the entrance from view. It looked more like it had split off from the rock around it, and tipped and slipped a little. It was probably there in Emma's time. Did she consider that the entrance, or was it the dark opening in the main cliff face?

Either way, she couldn't go too far wrong, even if she had to measure twice. Sam decided the opening in the cliff face was where Emma had measured from. She dug the tape out. Her mother had a rubber band around it to keep it neat. Sam slipped that off and promptly lost it in the dirt at her feet. No biggie.

Placing a rock on one end of the tape, Sam unrolled it to five feet. It was dark in there, and cold, but enough light came in that she could read the number on the tape. Now, halfway up the wall. She picked up the flashlight and ran the beam up and down the wall. There. She saw a rock sitting on a little outcrop. Someone had to have put it there. Sam's heart started pounding.

"Hellooooo? Sam, are you back there?"

"I think I found it."

She reached up and curled the fingers of her left hand over the top of the rock, planning to grab and move it. Before grabbing was an option she felt the wiry resistance of a spider web.

Jerking away like she'd been burnt, Sam gave a sharp cry and stumbled back. Her butt hit the floor of the cave hard. She'd dropped the flashlight, but found herself in a shaft of light coming in from the outside. Sam looked at her hands, turning them over and spreading her fingers. Then, she looked up and down her arms and frantically started patting her clothing.

"Sam, are you okay?" Hailey suddenly blocked most of the light.

Sam jumped up and stepped out of the main cave into the sunshine next to Hailey.

"Look!"

"What?"

"Look at my clothes; look in my hair!"

"Okay, okay. What am I looking for?"

"Spider!"

"Oh, for crying out..."

"Look! I didn't make fun of you about the snakes."

Hailey looked. She brushed Sam's back and parted her long, dirty-blond hair as if she were a monkey looking for nits. When she was satisfied, she told Sam so.

"Look *again*!"

She did. No spider. No nits.

"Where did you see it? You probably scared it and it ran off."

"In the cave, where the bottle is," Sam said. She paused for a moment before saying, "I didn't actually see it. I felt it, though. Felt its web." She shuddered.

"You didn't even see it?"

"No, but I…"

"Felt its web, right? Do you always freak out when you run into a spider web?"

"No, but this was different. This was a widow's web!"

"A black widow? How do you know?"

Sam kept combing through her hair as they talked.

"Because I know what they feel like. Dad killed one once in the garage and he had me feel the web so I would know the difference."

"What's so special about their webs?"

"They're really, really strong and stiff. It's like you can hear it when they tear."

"Huh," said Hailey. "I didn't know that. Where was it?"

"In there," Sam pointed. "Right where she said it was, about five feet in and halfway up the wall."

Hailey ducked into the opening and picked up the flashlight. Seconds later she emerged carrying a jar.

Sam's jaw dropped. "What about the spider?"

"You were right. It was a black widow. All shiny."

"So, you reached in anyway and grabbed the jar?"

"Basically. She scurried out of the way. It's not like they can fly or anything."

Sam glanced at the jar, then said, "C'mon."

"Where are we going?"

"Back to the road. I don't want to be anywhere near the

spider."

"She's clear back in..."

"Or the snakes."

Hailey looked down at the scattering of rocks around the entrance to the cave, then said, "Right."

Back on the road—in the center of the road, where they both agreed they were relatively safe from spiders and snakes—the girls examined the jar.

"Just like the first one," Hailey said.

"Except not broken. And, stamps!"

They could see a little square of four stamps looking perfectly preserved, resting on the bottom of the light blue bottle.

"There's something else in there," Sam said.

"Like what?"

"Looks like hair."

Chipping off the old, dried wax proved harder than they thought it would be. It took some work with the file part of a pair of fingernail clippers Hailey always carried with her. As the opener of the jar, she did the honors of reaching in and retrieving the stamps. She handed them to Sam, then stuck her hand back in the jar to get the other object.

"It is hair," Hailey said. "With a bright little pink ribbon tied around it."

"A lock of hair," Sam said. "Her hair."

At the realization they both stared for a long moment at the two-inch comma of blond hair resting in Hailey's hand.

"It could be yours," Hailey said. She held it up to Sam's tresses to compare. "Really. It's the same color."

***

The first thing they did when they got back to Sam's house was look up the value of stamps. They Googled "stamp values 1914" and instantly found what they were looking for.

"Whoa!" Hailey said. "Jackpot!"

"How much?" Sam asked.

Hailey pointed to the picture of a red, 2 cent stamp. "This one, right."

"I guess so. It looks exactly the same."

Hailey moved her finger down to the price.

"$240!? That's, like, each?"

"That's what it says."

"Do you think Beaker would pay that much?"

"Don't know. But, even if he paid half that you'd have enough for an iPhone."

***

Late that afternoon they rode their bikes to the teacher's house and dumped them down on the grass strip between the road and the sidewalk.

They walked up a faux brick walkway onto a concrete front step and rang the doorbell. In about 30 seconds the door opened. Sam was a little startled when she saw the teacher wearing a t-shirt for Bare Naked Ladies, a band she kind of liked.

"Yes?"

"Hi, Mr. Baker. We're..."

"No cookies," he said.

"Wait, what?"

"I don't need any cookies."

"I don't..." Then it dawned on her. "No, that's not... We're not selling cookies."

He looked them up and down as if checking for weapons.

"What are you selling?"

"Stamps!" Hailey said, giving him a cheerful smile.

"What next?" He said. "If the danged legislature would do better for the schools kids wouldn't have to pester people selling... stuff door-to-door. I don't need any stamps. I usually buy mine at the post office and I'm pretty sure you can't give me a better rate than they can."

He started to close the door.

"Stamp collector stamps," Sam said. "Like the ones you showed me and Dad when he bought that, whatever, from you last fall."

Baker kept the door open a crack.

"Collectables? Like what."

Sam took an envelope from her backpack, opened it and lifted out the crisp little four-stamp sheet. Baker opened the door far enough to get his head through and squinted at the stamps.

"1914? Where would you get something like this?"

Sam was prepared for this. "Well, you know about the Big House, the one my dad is always working on?"

"I know of it," Baker said. "The old Reed house out in the valley."

"That's the one. Did you know it was a post office once?"

"I did not."

"Well, it was. I don't know exactly when, but somewhere around the time these stamps were made."

"I see."

"Hailey and me have been helping Dad do some work there, and we found these stamps. I remembered seeing all your great stamps that time we were here, and I wondered if you'd be interested in these."

"Well," Baker said, "I could give them a good home if you don't want them."

"We were kind of hoping to sell them," Hailey said.

Baker twisted his mouth. "I see," he said again. After a moment he waived them into his house and pointed to a couple of chairs in his dining room. "Sit. I'll be right back."

He was gone for several minutes, giving Hailey and Sam time to take in his kitchen and dining room. Both were sparse and clean. The counters were free of newspapers and mail, the eternal piles that plagued the counters in the Reed home. There were a few dishes in a drying rack next to the sink. A Far Side calendar hung on one wall in the dining room. A plaster rooster key holder was mounted next to it, looking a little out of place.

When the teacher came back into the room, he said, "Yes, I think I could do something with these. How about $20?"

"Twenty dollars?" Hailey's tone was incredulous.

"For each of you, of course," Baker said.

Sam and Hailey's eyes met. Sam looked back at Baker.

"There's one thing we didn't mention," Sam said. "We know how much they're worth."

"Oh? How much do you think they're worth?"

"According to the Internet, they're worth $240 each."

"Well, you can't believe everything you see on the Internet, you girls know that."

"Yeah, we do," Hailey said. "That's why we checked more than one site. They're worth $240 apiece."

Baker's eyes moved back and forth from girl to girl. He seemed to consider.

"Two hundred dollars. That's the best I can do."

"Each?"

"Each? I was talking total."

"We're talking each," Hailey countered.

The stamps rested on the dining table on top of the envelope in which Sam had brought them. Baker gave the envelope a little push, then pulled it and the stamps closer to him.

"All right, I can go $200 each."

"Good," Hailey said. "But we were thinking $250."

"Each girl?"

"Of course, you just offered us $400 total. We wouldn't sell them for less."

"But..."

"Take it or leave it," Hailey said, reaching for the envelope.

"I..."

"They're worth twice that and you know it."

Baker thought about it for a minute, then said, "Would you take a check?"

"Gotta be cash," Hailey said.

Sam stared at her. Who was this girl?

Baker sighed. "I can get it for you tomorrow," he said.

***

June 21, 2014, nearly bedtime

We found it! We never would have seen the cave if it weren't for the tree. Well, what was left of the tree. It died a long time ago, but parts of the trunk were still there. We didn't see it at first, but when we finally found it, finding the cave was pretty easy. You were right about the bushes. They were really thick. They covered the cave completely.

Once we found the cave, finding the jar was easy. But there was a spider—a BLACK WIDOW!—had built a web around the bottle in the little hole thingy. I couldn't go near it, but Hailey did. She got the jar. AND the stamps! Thank you, thank you!

There was a lock of hair inside the jar with a little pink ribbon tied around it. That's your hair, right? You have pretty hair. Hailey says it looks just like mine, so OF COURSE it's pretty!

You asked why we need stamps. Not to mail a letter, though we still do mail letters, sometimes. I mean, not me, but some people. My dad gets bills and stuff. Mostly I text people. Which, you're not going to understand, but it's the reason I need the stamps. Wow, this gets confusing. You probably think we need stamps to send a text. We don't. I don't. I need a phone. The phone I need is not like the phones you probably know about. The phone I need doesn't hang on a wall and it doesn't need a cord. I know this probably sounds all weird to you, but our phones are small. I'm trying to think of something you would know about so I could tell you how small. A change purse? Half a sandwich? About that small. We carry them in our pockets or in a purse if we don't have pockets.

Now, this part is going to sound really, really weird. We can use our phones to talk with other people—with our voices. We don't do that much, though. We mostly send texts. Those are very short messages. Maybe a sentence or two. Our phones have tiny keyboards that we can use to enter the messages.

Anyway, my phone got, well, wet. So it doesn't work anymore. I need a new one and they are very expensive. Like, $500. That's why the stamps. The stamps you sent me... You didn't exactly send them, did you? The stamps you left for me in the jar are valuable now because they are so old. Stamp collectors will pay a lot of money for them. We're getting $500 from this guy tomorrow! Then I can get a new iPhone! So, thank you, thank you!

Your new BFF,

Sam

JUNE 2014

Sunday	Monday	Tuesday	Wednesday	Thursday	Friday	Saturday
1	2	3	4	5	6	7
8	9	10	11	12	13	14
15 B Day!	16	17	18	19	20	21
22	23	24	25	26	27	28 Duke Dies
29	30					

June 22, 1914

Trying to understand what you are telling me makes me want to take a powder. First, I think you must mean telephone when you say "phone." It seems you must, though what you describe is outlandish. You are in the future, so I trust that what you say about them being so small & that they do not need a cord. It sounds so strange. Does your sink need pipes, or does water flow magically from the air?

Then, at the end, you call it an "iPhone." Still, I think you mean telephone. Is this a different kind? Why would you spell it that way and why is the capital letter second? "Texts." That is another thing I understand half of at best. I know textbooks. Is a text something written, then, or printed? I imagine a page of this diary torn out and put into a telephone. Would it fall out of a telephone belonging to someone else, then? How do you get it into the telephone? And out?

As I said, I will consider you the expert on the future, since you live there. I guess.

Stamps! How can it be that four stamps are worth $500? They cost 8 cents now. Is everyone in the future so rich they just throw money away? You said a collector would pay you that much. So their value is that they are so old? The stamps that are brand new right now are old and valuable in your time.

It pleases me that you are so happy with the stamps. Should I send more? The stamps are still here, in the ice cave. Should I put more in the jar? But, no. If I had done that, you would have mentioned that there were more. Wouldn't you? The jar is here, now, but in your time it is in your house and you have already opened it. I may need two powders!

Maybe I could hide another jar. I could buy a few more stamps. For pennies I could make you rich girls. That makes me laugh! I wish you could send something back to me! Maybe you could send a "phone" and we could talk to each other!

I just reread what you wrote & found another word that means something to me, but I think it means something different to you. I have seen a key board before. At least, I think I have. There is a hotel in town & it has a board nailed to the wall where they hang keys to all the rooms. Is that what you meant? How would that help you send messages?

My head hurts thinking about all this. I am really going to get that powder, now.

Emma

Sam sent Hailey an email.

"Got another one. can you come over after sup?"

Using a full-size keyboard felt clunky and ancient.

Sam smiled to herself. It was funny that Emma thought

they were in a hotel, or something. She could not assume the girl would know what words meant.

"*Sure*," came Hailey's reply a couple of minutes later.

Email was like texting, but it definitely was not texting. Hailey was keeping an eye on her email, something she normally checked about once a week, if she remembered at all. Still, it wasn't the instant back and forth they were used to. Emailing was for dinosaurs.

***

That evening, Hailey closed the door to Sam's room behind them. Sam put her finger to her lips.

"What?" Hailey asked.

Sam slipped her hand into a pillow sham on her bed and brought out five bills.

"Whoa!"

Sam spread them out like a hand of cards, showing that each was a hundred dollar bill.

"Whoa!" Hailey, repeated.

Sam tucked the bills back in her pillow.

"So, that's for the stamps?"

Sam nodded. "I rode over and got it this afternoon."

"Cool. Did he give you any grief?"

"Not really. He said he might be interested in more."

"Do you think we could get more?"

"Read the diary," Sam said, pushing it toward Hailey.

Hailey read the entry, laughing a couple of times.

"We've got her a little confused, don't we?" She asked.

"That's fair," Sam said. "She's confusing me just as much. What's this 'take a powder?'"

Hailey said, "That's, like, from gangster movies or something, isn't it? Did you look it up?"

"Duh," Sam said. She slipped into her desk chair and started hitting keys.

"It says…" She worked her lips without sound coming out for a couple of seconds. "Yeah, gangster movies. Something about leaving town. Maybe when you were in trouble. Wait." Sam's lips started moving again. "This makes more sense. They don't know where the saying came from, exactly, but people around Emma's time said it a lot. They weren't talking about leaving town. It was, like, they were taking an aspirin. I guess before pills, you took a little packet of powder."

"So, we're giving her a headache?"

"That's what it says. It's what she said, actually."

"That whole keyboard thing was hilarious. Does she think we rent out rooms?"

"Yeah, we'll need to explain that to her."

"And, order more stuff!" Hailey said.

There was a knock on the door. It opened before either of them could say anything.

"Hey, dweebs," Rachel said, closing the door behind her.

Sam closed her browser window. That sudden move did not go unnoticed.

"What are you up to? Looking at porn?"

"Porn? Ewww," said Hailey.

Sam clicked on her browser icon and the page popped back up again. Rachel glanced at it.

"Wikipedia? That's worse than porn. You guys learning stuff or something?"

"Just messing around," Sam said. She didn't know why she'd even closed the thing.

"Whatevs," Rachel said. "Hey, twerp, I heard they might have an opening at the Big Bun."

Sam squinted at her, as if Rachel were out of focus.

"A job, ditz," Rachel said. "You wanted to earn money for a phone, right?"

"Oh, yeah," Sam said. She really hadn't thought about a job for a while. She didn't think she needed one.

"So, you going to apply?"

Sam shrugged. "Maybe."

"Maybe? Dad's not going to give you money for a phone. Are you resigned to living in the last century?"

"No, I need a phone."

"Well, job, money, phone."

"I've already..."

Hailey interrupted. "So, we were thinking about helping your dad, right?"

"Yeah, we were thinking about that," Sam said.

Rachel made a poofing sound with lips. "That'll take forever. He's going to pay you, like, eleven cents an hour."

That's when Sam blurted out, "I've already got enough for a phone." The minute she said it she regretted it.

"You do?"

Sam nodded.

"How did you...?"

"Doesn't matter."

"You didn't steal it, did you?"

Hailey said, "We didn't steal it."

"Well, how did you get that much money?"

"Trust me, Rach, we didn't do anything wrong. It's not like we sold our bodies, or anything."

"No shit," Rachel said. "Who'd give money for those?"

Both Sam and Hailey stuck their tongues out at her.

"So, really, where did you get it?"

"It's a secret," Sam said. "But, I have $500."

"No way," Rachel said.

"Way." Sam reached behind her sister, who was sitting on the bed, and pulled the bills from her pillow sham.

"This is my new iPhone," Sam said, holding them up and giving them a little shake.

Rachel looked at them, her mouth hanging open.

"What'd you guys do, rob a bank?"

"None of your beeswax," Hailey said. It was a favorite expression of her mother, which made her blush the minute she said it.

"So, are you printing this stuff?"

"It's real," Sam said. For an instant she wondered if you actually could scan dollars and print them off. Uh, no, probably not.

"But, you'll still need a job."

"Why? This will get me an iPhone. Maybe the latest model."

"Maybe, but there's tax and stuff."

"Okay, maybe not the latest model, but the one that's almost the latest."

"Sure, you can buy a phone, but what about service?"

"Waddaya mean?"

"How are you going to pay the monthly bill?"

Sam's eyes widened like she'd just been slapped.

"Won't your dad pay?" Hailey asked.

"No way," said Rachel.

"But he paid for the old one," Sam said.

"Yeah, and you dumped it in the toilet," said Rachel. "He's POed about that. He's not going to pay for it anymore, at least not all of it. I heard him and Mom talking. They want you to have a stake in it so you're more careful."

"I'll be more careful," Sam said. Even she heard the whiny tone in her voice.

"So you say," Rachel said. "And, anyway, how are you going to explain where you got the money? Where did you get the money?"

Sam avoided that question. She said, "We can get more. A lot more, if we need it."

"Really? What are you little tramps doing?"

"We're not tramps," Hailey said. "This is legit."

"Yeah, I'll bet. But even if you can get more money, they're not going to sell you service. You've got to have a checking account or a credit card."

"You do?" Sam asked. "Even if you've got money?"

"Yes, frog face, they need a credit card."

For a moment, Sam was silent. Then she said, "You've got a credit card, right?"

"Oh no. No way! I'm not letting you use my credit

card."

"But I'm your little sister that you love so much."

"Mom and Dad would flip if they found out. They'd take my card away, which would mean I'd probably lose my phone, which is totally not going to happen."

***

Sam had pleaded with Rachel, listing—as best she could remember—the countless, or at least the several good deeds she had done for her older sister. Rachel didn't budge. She did try to get the girls to tell her where they got the money. The girls didn't budge.

The conversation ended in stalemate when Rachel threw up her hands and left the room.

"That was fun," Hailey said.

"It sucked," said Sam.

"Oh, she'll get over it."

"Or tell Mom and Dad about the money."

Hailey said, "I don't think she'll do that. Girl code, you know."

"Girl code?"

"Yeah, like we wouldn't tell on her. That sort of thing."

Sam sighed. "Maybe." She started to stuff the money back in her pillow sham, then decided against it. She had a picture of she and Rachel and her parents propped on the nightstand. Sam grabbed that and took the back off. She smoothed the bills out and popped the back into the frame, swinging the little tabs to hold it in.

"We should write her back," Hailey said. "You could ask for more stamps."

"What's the point? She can't send me a credit card."

"Yeah, but it's still money. You can always use money." Hailey paused for a moment. "We could always use money."

Sam looked at her. She remembered how Hailey had pressured Beaker to give them more money. Sam couldn't have done that on her own. They had told Beaker the money was for both of them, yet Sam had kept it all for her phone.

"I guess we could," Sam said. "This time, the money is yours."

"Cool! Makeup!"

***

June 22, 2014

So, hiding another jar for us is a good idea. More stamps, please. The same kind are fine. Other kinds if you can get them.

We wanted to explain that a keyboard isn't a place to keep keys. I mean, it could be, but that's not what we're talking about. You have typewriters back then, right? I know you do because it says on Wiki Anyway, we read that you have typewriters. We're talking about those kind of keys. A keyboard looks like a typewriter, with all the letters and everything. You touch the letters to make words, like on a typewriter. Only, you use your thumbs. We use our thumbs. If you type, you probably use most of your fingers. It's easier for us to use our thumbs because the keypad, keyboard, is very, very tiny.

Okay, what else? The phone. Never mind about the phone, for now. That's a problem because I don't have a cr a good way to pay for service. I can pay for the phone, but it costs to use it. That's what I don't have a good way for. I can't pay for it the way they want cause I'm just a teenager.

Last time, I got the money from selling the stamps. This time, Hailey gets it, because that's fair. She already has a phone, so she'll probably buy makeup.

Hailey is asking me to ask you if you have makeup. Of course you do, though maybe you're too young to use it. I bet your mom has some. Hailey is asking again about makeup. She wants to know if you can put some lip gloss in the jar. You'd call it lipstick, I think. Can you do that?

Thanks,

Your friends Sam and the Makeup Queen (Hailey)

"We should probably be asking more about her," Hailey said.

"You think?"

"It's kind of all about us."

Sam squinched up a corner of her mouth. "You're probably right. We'll ask if she has pets or something next time."

JUNE 2014

Sunday	Monday	Tuesday	Wednesday	Thursday	Friday	Saturday
	2	3	4	5	6	7
8	9	10	11	12	13	14
15 B Day	16	17	18	19	20	21
22	23	24	25	26	27	28 Duke Dies
29	30					

The first thing Sam did when she got up the next morning was check to see that the bills were still in the back of the picture frame. They were.

The next thing she did was check the diary. Better than email, there was another entry.

June 23, 1914

I will buy some more stamps, though I do not have $500! I have a few pennies that I can spare. I would rather buy candy or save up for a dime novel.

As it happens, I have a tube of lipstick that I can put in a jar. Can you believe it? I had never seen one until my cousin Florence came to stay with us for a few days a couple of weeks ago. She is 17 and talks about boys a lot. My mother says she uses too much makeup, though she does not say it to her.

Florence left a few days earlier than planned because she was feeling weak. I think she packed in a hurry, because she left some things. I found a small hair comb when I went to clean her room. I also found the lipstick. I have a little confession about that. I gave the comb to Mother, but I kept the lipstick. It is a metal tube with a little metal piece on the side that you slide to make the lipstick come out. But you know that, I suppose.

I will put stamps & the lipstick in another jar and seal it with wax as I did the last. I feel a little naughty about something else. I tried the lipstick and looked in the mirror. Oh, I won't be wearing that again soon! I was going to wipe it right off. My mother came in the room just then so I licked it off, instead. I told you I am naughty!!!

I hid the lipstick, thinking I would give it back to Florence someday. She has not written to ask about it. She has been ill ever since she left and has not written at all. Her mother sent a note telling how worried they are about her.

So, I think it is safe to send that lipstick into the future. I will not be wearing it & I do not think Florence would much care if she never saw it again.

When I looked for a hiding place for the first jar, I found another cranny that might work about three feet to the right and near the floor. I did not choose that one because the jar kept tumbling forward. I will find some rocks to prop it up and some rocks to put in front.

I won't be able to resist looking at the first jar. It will still be there, won't it? Of course it will, because even though you've found it, you HAVE NOT FOUND IT. YOU ARE NOT EVEN BORN YET!!! Funny!

Your Emma

PS: What is a "teenager"?

***

"C'mon!" Hailey shouted back at Sam. "You pedal like an old woman!"

"Yeah, yeah," Sam muttered. Hailey was much more eager to retrace their trip. She seemed to have forgotten about the snakes given the promise of both money and lipstick. Sam, meanwhile, had not forgotten about the spider. In her mind it was lurking in the cave waiting for her return. She'd had that dream again last night. The bad one. It made her wonder if the spider in the cave had spent all its time building a gigantic web, doubling and tripling each strand until it was strong as steel.

By the time they had ridden past the big house and up the valley to the hilltop overlooking the house where they had met the woman, Sam was about worn out. Hailey had slowed some, but gave no sign of stopping.

"Wait!" Sam called.

Hailey skidded in the gravel ahead of her and put a foot down.

"What?"

"Let's stop here for a minute," Sam said. "I want to think."

"You can't think while you ride?"

Sam ignored her and said, "I just want to get our story straight, in case we run into that woman, again, or maybe someone else."

"What story?" Hailey asked. "We liked the rock writing, so we're coming back to look at it again."

"I suppose, but that sounds a little lame."

Hailey rolled her eyes. "We're taking pictures. For a school report."

"It's summer."

"Like it's always going to be summer? We're going to report on what we did on our vacation, okay?"

That didn't sound awful, though Sam couldn't remember doing that since about the fourth grade.

"Besides, we might not even see anyone."

Sam studied the farmyard below them. It didn't look any different from the last time they were here, except there wasn't a sprinkler running and no one was in the front yard. There weren't any cars in sight, either.

"Okay," Sam said, stepping up on her pedal and moving forward. "You do the talking this time."

"I'm good at that," said Hailey, and started off again.

They rode through the dusty area in front of the yard. There was a little gravel there and several sets of car tracks. Still no cars. No pickups, either, Sam thought. This was a farm. They probably had pickups.

The girls rode around behind the outbuildings and found the dirt road leading to the rock writing. This time, they knew right where they were going. They stopped and dropped their bikes into the dirt. Hailey started up through the cheat grass. She stopped.

"You wouldn't mind going first, would you?" Hailey asked.

So she hadn't forgotten about the snakes.

"I'll make a deal with you," Sam said. "I'll go first all the way to the cave. You go first into the cave. In fact, you go into the cave, period. I don't want to get near it."

"Scaredy," Hailey said, grinning at her.

"Snakes," Sam said.

The girls regarded each other for a moment. Then, Hailey nodded and Sam stepped by her.

Crawling under the brush was easier this time. It grabbed and snagged a little less and Sam was through it in a few seconds. When she stood up and turned, Hailey was right behind her.

Sam put one hand on the warm rock and leaned around it to peer into the opening of the cave.

"I don't suppose snakes would like it in there," Hailey said, from behind her.

"Nah, they'd be out in the sun," Sam said. She didn't have a clue if that was right or not. "They're cold-blooded, remember? They like the heat."

Hailey seemed predisposed to accept any argument that would help her reach the makeup. She pulled a tiny LED flashlight from her pack and ducked through the opening.

For a long moment, Sam heard nothing from inside the cave. Then, there came a scraping and brushing sounds.

"Where's the spider?"

"Who cares?" replied Hailey, from inside the cave. "I'm looking for lipstick."

More brushing and the sound of pebbles tossed across the floor of the cave.

"Bingo!"

"Spider?"

"Jar, dipshit. I found it!"

In seconds Hailey was out of the cave and into the light holding up another glass bottle.

"It's wet," said Sam.

"Just the outside, I think. There was ice all around it. It was frozen into a bunch of gravel clear back in a corner on the floor of the cave."

Hailey used the tail of her t-shirt to wipe off a little sheen of moisture. They could see inside, now. There was a small sheet of six or eight stamps and a shape that looked like it might be a lipstick tube.

"Should we open it?" Hailey asked.

"No. Let's get it back to the house."

***

By the time they got back to Sam's room, the jar was not the least bit cold. Hailey used her fingernail file to chip away at the old wax. She tried opening the bottle without success. Then, Hailey wrapped a bit of Sam's bedspread around the lid so she could get a better grip. She strained and it finally broke free.

Hailey dumped the contents out onto the bedspread. There were eight stamps. That would be $1,000, if they were as valuable as the first ones. Hailey ignored them and picked up the lipstick. She stood up and went to a small, decorative mirror Sam had on one wall. There were a couple of pictures and an old Jr. High ID card stuck between the frame and the glass. Hailey started running the lipstick over her lips.

"Yuck. It's kind of chalky."

"What did you expect? It's a hundred years old."

Hailey rubbed at it with her fingers, trying to spread it evenly across her bottom lip, then her top. It wasn't working well. She licked her lips and smacked them together, then moved them back and forth trying to get a good, smooth coat. Better, but still a little lumpy.

"That sucks," Hailey said. She turned her head, tilting it from side to side, studying her reflection. "Sucks," she said, again. Hailey pulled a Kleenex from the box next to Sam's bed and began wiping the lipstick away.

"So, you'll buy some. You're rich, you know."

"Yeah, if Beaker's still good for it."

JUNE 2014

Sunday	Monday	Tuesday	Wednesday	Thursday	Friday	Saturday
1	2	3	4	5	6	7
8	9	10	11	12	13	14
15 B'Day!	16	17	18	19	20	21
22	23	24	25	26	27	28 Duke Dies
29	30					

June 24, 1914

I wonder what has happened? I hid the new jar, as I said I would. Did you find it? Am I too impatient? For me, a day has passed. For you a hundred years. But, no, it has been just a day for you, hasn't it? You read my words yesterday, I assume. Would you have had time to visit the cave and retrieve the jar? I know so little about your lives. Sometimes I think you must fly from place to place like the Wright brothers. Do you have your own airplanes?

Your not writing should not disturb me. You must have things that keep you from it. You probably go to dances and fairs. Do you still have moving pictures?

But it does disturb me that you did not write. I think of the story you told me about going into the cave to find the first jar & encountering a terrible spider. Could I have sent you to your death by spider bite? Or could the roof of the cave come tumbling down onto you?

You <u>must</u> write! Now that I believe you exist, I want you to continue to exist.

Your worried one,

Emma

***

June 24, 2014

Sorry, sorry. I should have written before going to sleep last night. I was so tired from riding to the cave, again. And, yes, we did go there. Yes, we found the other jar. It's like Christmas getting presents from the past. Wow, I just thought of how that word—present—has two meanings. It can be a gift and it can be a time. My present is your future and your present is my past, or anyway the past. But we're writing like our presents are together. I feel like they really are.

We got the stamps, so Hailey is rich! Thanks! I'm going over to her house today to learn more about you. Isn't that weird? Hailey's mother is a Mormon—do you have Mormons where when you lived? I spose. Anyway, they have this thing where they try to learn all about their relatives and keep track of them so everybody can go to heaven. Really. I'm like, whatever, but Hailey's mom is really into it. So, we're going to learn some stuff about you.

Gees, I feel like a fortune teller! I can tell you when you're going to meet a tall, dark handsome man! I'll know how many kids you'll have, if you have kids. Stuff like that.

Anyway, got to go. Sorry, again, for not writing. I didn't mean to worry you.

Your Future Friend,

Sam.

***

An invitation to Hailey's house was rare. She always preferred to meet somewhere else so she could escape her parents and siblings. Her parents—her units—were strict about not using makeup and not dating until Hailey was 16. In those ways, they weren't much different from Sam's parents. They went to church a *lot* more. A lot more. Sam's mom and dad never really went, unless it was for a funeral or a wedding. Her mom's parents were Episcopalian and her dad's were sort of Lutheran. Neither Chris nor Amanda Reed talked much about religion, and they let their girls decide for themselves what to believe. Not Hailey's parents. They were devout Mormons and expected Hailey to follow that path. The more they pushed, the more she resisted. There was a constant tension in the house about it, with Hailey balking at every effort to involve her in the church and her parents trying to persuade her to participate.

Every time Sam saw the Poulsen house she marveled at how many people called it home. It was an average-sized house, with three bedrooms, one for Mr. and Mrs. Poulsen; one for Hailey and her older sister, Hannah; and one for the boys; Taylor, 6; Joel, 7; Jacob, 10; and Aaron, 12. The youngest Poulsen was Brendie, who was 8 months old and still slept in her parent's room.

Seven kids. Sam couldn't imagine having six siblings. She didn't have to imagine it. Hailey kept her well informed about what it was like. For one thing, it was like a hospital ward. Someone was always getting sick, and when one of them got sick, they all got sick, eventually. Usually just colds and stuff. Nobody ever got anything really serious. Which was a special point that Mrs. Poulsen often made. She didn't believe in vaccines, so none of the kids ever got shots. Mrs. Poulsen—Mr. Poulsen, too, Sam guessed— was afraid the kids would catch something from the vaccinations, or end up with autism. Hailey always had to bring a note from her parents explaining that she could not get shots because of religious reasons, or something. Which was okay with Hailey. She practically passed out if you'd even say anything about needles.

Sam had asked Hailey about why her family didn't believe in getting shots. Her answer made some kind of sense to Sam. "Because those diseases are dead," Hailey had said. "Who gets smallpox anymore? Or measles? Nobody gets polio. So what's the point?"

Sam Googled it up one night when she was bored, she found there was a raging debate about it on the internet. Duh. Like, what wasn't there a raging debate about on the internet? The anti-vaxxers were worried about autism and mercury. They were worried that kids got too many shots all at once. The pro side said the science was clear: Vaccines saved lives and they were safe. Well, pretty safe. Bad things sometimes happened, like one in kazillion times or something, but that wasn't near as bad as getting one of the diseases.

Sam read about something called "herd immunity." That word "herd" bothered her, like humans were cattle, or something. The idea was that when most people had immunity through vaccination, it was harder for disease to spread, so people who didn't get vaccinations were making it riskier for everyone, not just themselves.

But were the diseases "dead," as Hailey said? Smallpox was. Measles was still around, though, and so was polio. Mostly not in the United States, though, so maybe Hailey was right.

None of the other Mormon kids skipped vaccinations, as far as Sam knew, so the reason they skipped shots was not really religious. It was just one more thing that set the Poulsens apart. They were Mormon, but just a little more Mormon than everyone else. It was like they knew a whole bunch of stuff no one else did. Or, at least they thought they knew it. It made them seem a little more virtuous, which was not an attractive feature, in Sam's opinion.

Hailey's 17-year-old sister, often called The Ice Queen, by Hailey, was the most notably righteous of the kids. She never missed a church function, and there were many. Hannah was the pride of her parents, accepting their wise supervision without complaint and the word of God without question.

It was Sam's theory that if Hailey were born first, the Poulsens might have stopped having kids right there. Hailey thrived on trouble, with a lower case t. She wasn't a bad kid, just a mischievous one. Mrs. Poulsen went on and on about what a troublesome child Hailey had been, always into things and taking every "no" as a challenge. Hailey was easily bored. Never more so than when it came to church functions. Nevertheless, Mrs. P. insisted that she participate in everything. At first. Hailey had a talent for irritating the brothers and sisters of the church, who, while openly welcoming, made it clear that they did not much mind when Hailey stayed home.

In spite of their seemingly ongoing failure in raising Hailey well, the Poulsens had taken comfort in their perfect oldest child and decided to have a third. Aaron was a sweet kid, every bit as perfect as Hannah. So, Jacob came along. He was a little rougher around the edges, but that did not dissuade them from bringing Joel and Taylor and Brendie into the world.

Brendie was a surprise to Sam. She thought Hailey's family was complete when Taylor was born six years earlier. Mrs. Poulsen was only a year younger than her own mother. The thought of her mother getting pregnant kind of creeped Sam out.

Hailey, meanwhile, was shocked at the birth of Brendie, not because her mother had another child, but because she had a girl child. She was expecting another little brother. Four in a row seemed like a trend. It wasn't that Hailey did not like her newborn sister. She was looking forward to having her room all to herself when Hannah went to BYU next year. Now, she'd have to share it with a toddler.

Sam ditched her bike and hopped up on the front stoop to rap on the door. She heard the pounding of feet. The door opened to reveal two boys, Taylor and Joel, Taylor in a t-shirt and underpants and Joel in pajamas. Without any greeting they turned as one and screamed, "Hailey!" The boys thundered away and down the hall.

Hannah flounced past the door, dressed in a long dress

with puffy sleeves. She gave Sam a little smile that seemed to say, "I know so much more than you."

Finally, Hailey appeared and ushered her in.

"C'mon. Mom's in the sewing room."

The sewing room was also home to an ironing board, an ancient boom box, and the family computer. Hailey had her own laptop, which to Sam was nothing short of amazing. No one had their own anything in this house.

"Hello, Sammy."

"Hi, Mrs. Poulsen."

"It's so nice to have you over for a change."

Sam smiled at her.

"Well," Mrs. Poulsen said, "I suppose you want to see what we've found out."

"Yes, Ma'am."

"I think it's wonderful for a young person to take interest in their family," Mrs. Poulsen said. "How is your family, by the way?"

"They're fine."

"Rachel home from school?"

"Yes, she is."

"What's she studying? Does she have a boyfriend?"

Sam was tempted to say that Rachel was studying boys. "Communications," she said.

"Isn't that nice? Wants to work for a newspaper, I suppose."

Maybe, if this were the 1950s, Sam thought.

"Mom," Hailey intervened. "Can we show her the family tree stuff."

"Genealogy, dear. Of course. Come sit on this footstool, Samantha."

Sam did. Hailey put one hand on the desk and leaned over the monitor. It was the biggest monitor Sam had ever seen. Big in all the wrong ways. It was the old style with the vented plastic back that looked like it could house chickens. It probably weighed more than she did. Yet, the screen wasn't much bigger than a laptop's.

"So, we're on the Ancestry site. Are you familiar with that?"

"Not really," said Sam.

"Well, it will do so many things. Give you hints about your relatives, help you look through old Social Security records and old newspapers, help you find photos."

"Hints?" Sam asked. This sounded a little like a game.

"They call it that because they're only possibilities. The computer—aren't they the most amazing things? The computer finds things that might relate to your relatives." Mrs. Poulsen grinned, as if that were some kind of joke. "You have to go look at whatever it is and decide if it really is about some person in your family. It usually isn't, but when it is, what fun!"

"Mom..."

"Be patient, dear. I'm getting there."

Sam said, "I appreciate your doing this, Mrs. Poulsen."

"Oh, my word, it isn't anything! I just love helping people with genealogy. You know, it's important to us in our church."

"Yes, I'd... Hailey told me about that."

"Well, Hailey isn't exactly an expert," said Mrs. Poulsen. "But I suppose she told you the general drift. We want to make sure all our relatives are baptized, especially those who didn't get a chance to hear the Word of the Lord."

"Mom..."

"Oh, be patient for once. It's right here. Now," she said, finger on the screen, "this is you. See, it has your birth date in 2000. And there's your older sister."

The screen showed a bunch of beige boxes, all the same size, with lines going between them. Most boxes had a tiny photo of the person represented, plus the years of their birth and death, if they were dead. Sam noticed her box had a girl's silhouette in pink instead of a picture. Boys or men without pictures got a silhouette of a man on a field of blue.

"And here are your parents, Chris and Amanda," continued Mrs. Poulsen. She moved her finger up a line and said, "And these are your grandparents on your father's side, Charles and Maxine." She frowned. "Just the three boys?"

The question was clearly for her, but Sam wasn't sure what she meant.

"Three boys?"

"Yes, you have two uncles but no aunts on your father's side, right?"

"Yeah, that's right."

"Shame," said Mrs. Poulsen. She moved her finger up a level and said, "Here's your great-grandparents on your father's side. Everything we're looking at will be on your father's side, today. Unless you'd like to explore your mother's side of the family, too."

"Uh, no thanks. Maybe another time."

"You can do a lot of this on your own, you know. It is a little expensive to get the whole package. A teenager couldn't afford it, but there is an awful lot for free. I'll give you the website address."

"Mom, she can find a website," Hailey said.

"Anyway, here are your grandparents, James and Agnes Reed."

Sam noticed that James Reed was born in 1913. That meant he was a baby in Emma's time. The time of the diary.

"James' parents—your great-grandparents—were Robert and Ethel Reed, the people in this picture. See?"

She did see. Robert was dressed in a stogy suit that showed a pocket watch chain. He had a long beard. His wife, Ethel, wore a bun and had a locket of some kind pinned to her dress.

"Now," Mrs. Poulsen said, "we need to double click on James to find what you're looking for. There she is. Shame there isn't a picture."

There were the siblings, James, John, George, Virginia and... Emma. There was only a bit of information about Emma. Just enough to turn Sam's blood cold. Birth: June 12, 1900 Death: June 30, 1914.

***

Hailey led Sam to the room Hailey shared with her sister. They passed the boys' bedroom. It smelled like hamsters lived there.

They shut the door behind them and sat on Hailey's

bed, on Hailey's side of the room. There was no line down the middle. Hailey differentiated her side with posters, the far edge of which was the demarcation. Three were for boy bands, five featured blond teen rock girls dressed in such a way that it must have given Mrs. Poulsen a heart murmur, and the rest were a mix of movie posters, demotivational posters, and quotes from famous people. She had not skipped the ceiling.

Meanwhile, Hannah's side of the room had its posters. One was a "Hang in there baby!" cat poster. The other one was a somber painting of Jesus. Her bed was neatly made covered with stuffed animals.

Sam had seen it all before and wouldn't have taken any notice in any case. She wasn't noticing much outside of her churning head.

"She's *dead*!?" Sam whispered, when they plopped down on the bed.

"Yeah, you knew that, right?"

"Of course, I knew she was dead. But, I mean she's dead then. Or, she's about to be dead. My god, we've got to tell her!"

"Tell her?" Hailey said. "Tell her what?"

"To watch out," Sam said. "Or, maybe to not go to town the day she's going to be hit by a bus. I don't know. We have to do something!"

"We don't even know how she dies. I asked Mom. She couldn't find anything. It only has the date."

In a tiny voice, Sam said, "I was going to tell her when she'd meet her husband."

***

Sam went through the rest of the day in a fog. She could not keep her mind on anything in the present. She was lost in the past. The inevitable past. She would owe Emma another entry, soon. What would she say? Sam wanted to warn her, but then reminded herself that she could not change the past. Emma had been dead nearly a hundred years. Even if she could change the past, should she? Having Emma live was surely a good thing, wasn't it?

Sam thought of a list of reasons why it might not turn out so well. Emma might grow up, get married and have a husband who beat her. Or, she might die some long, horrible death much worse than the one that now faced her. Maybe she would have kids and one of them would end up being a serial killer. Or, maybe a presidential assassin.

Sam drove those negative thoughts from her mind with positive ones. Emma's child would find a cure for cancer, or be president of the United States. Emma herself would become a brilliant inventor because she would know exactly what to invent. She would get rich, because Sam would tell her how. Emma would be a famous stock speculator who was never wrong, which would mean the whole family would become rich.

Except the whole family wasn't rich. They didn't have a famous inventor in their line and there was no presidential cousin. There was only Emma's death. It chilled Sam to think it, but Emma had to die. She had to die because she had died.

Changing the past would change the future. Sam lived

in the future, so the risks were great.

***

That evening, after supper, Sam spent a little time on the genealogy site. She had a hunger to know more about this girl from the past.

Emma was born in 1900. They knew that, already. She was the oldest of the family of five children. Her brother, John, was two years younger. Brother George was born in 1906. Virginia, who went by Virgie, was born in 1910 and James—Sam's grandfather—was born in 1913.

Some of the dates shocked Sam. John was already dead. Already, in the sense that Emma was writing in 1914. John had died of pneumonia in 1908, when he was about six. George would live only until 1928. He would marry, but die before having any children. Virgie married a man named Nelson. They had three children. One was named Florence. It was a name Sam recognized. She thought it was "Aunt" Florence, who was really her great aunt. She even remembered her, a little. She died when Sam was seven.

Emma seemed the most real of them all because Sam knew her. Kind of. Yet, it was James Reed and his marriage to Agnes Marie Welton in 1934 that was really most important. They had a son named Charles, in 1937, who married Mary Maxine Pratt. Charles and Mary were her grandparents on her father's side.

So, Emma's little brother, James, was Sam's grandfather. She'd never mentioned having a little brother, had she? Who had she mentioned?

Sam picked up the diary and skimmed the most recent

passage. There was a name there, wasn't there? Yes, Florence. Could that be Aunt Florence? Had Sam actually known someone who knew Emma?

Back on the website she did a search for the name Florence. Two hits came up in her family tree. The first was for Florence Gilbert Reed, born in 1897, who died in 1914. That couldn't be Aunt Florence. There was also a Florence Nelson, born in 1932. That was Sam's great aunt. Sam vaguely remembered the name Nelson. And, yes, that Florence died in 2007

Okay, so she hadn't met Emma's Florence. Wait. What was that death date, again, the one for Emma's Florence? Sam repeated the search and clicked through to the information page on Florence Gilbert Reed. If this was Emma's cousin... Relationships made Sam's hair follicles hurt, but she thought it through and followed the links back to find that Florence's father and Emma's father were brothers. So, that made Emma Rose Reed and Florence Gilbert Reed cousins. This had to be her.

Sam looked up the death date for Florence. June 28, 1914. That was, like, five days away! Well, six days and a hundred years in the past. Emma didn't know her cousin was about to die. Should she tell her?

Then, Sam remembered. Emma was about to die just two days after her cousin. What was the point?

Sam clicked a tab for pictures of Florence. There were three of them. One showed her as a baby in a tiny rocking chair. It had wrinkles in it like someone had carried it in a wallet. In another, Florence looked like she was about 10 or 11. She was standing next to a rope swing. The third was when she was about 17 or 18, standing with a younger girl on the front step of a house, framed by decorative pillars. Sam recognized those pillars. She could just make out the head of a lion. The picture had been taken in front of the Big House. A note said, "Florence Gilbert Reed, circa 1914 with unidentified girl."

Unidentified, maybe. But Sam knew who it was.

JUNE 2014

Sunday	Monday	Tuesday	Wednesday	Thursday	Friday	Saturday
	2	3	4	5	6	7
8	9	10	11	12	13	14
15 B Day!	16	17	18	19	20	21
22	23	24	25	26	27	28 Duke Dies
29	30 She Dies					

Sam had gone to sleep without writing in the diary. She had not even opened it to see if Emma had answered her last message.

It struck Sam that it was no longer a diary. It was more like texting or sending emails. Weird that what her dad said about the diary the day he gave it to her had really come true. He tried to convince her it did a lot of the same things an iPhone would do. What would he think if he knew it could do some things even an iPhone couldn't, like send messages back and forth between the past and the present?

Sam got out of bed, took the diary from her bookshelf and opened it to find the following.

June 25, 1914

Oh, I am so <u>relieved</u> that there is nothing wrong! Silly me. I got myself into quite a state worrying about it. I nearly made myself sick! I think maybe I did. I do not feel well this morning. The worry stole my energy, I think. I can barely hold *my pen.*

Sam stopped reading there and looked up. Her eyes fell on the deck of the tree house just outside of her window, but they did not register it. Emma was sick! It had already started, whatever she had would take her life in five days.

It makes me happy to know I made someone in the future rich!!! To think that little me, a silly girl, could change things in the future in such a wonderful way!

Two things I must comment on from your most recent words. First, yes, we have Mormons. Many of them. Mother says too many. I am not so sure. They seem nice enough to me.

The second thing is about your "ride" to the ice cave. What did you ride? If I went there I would just walk. Not today, but on a day when I felt better. Maybe I would ride my horse. Do you have a horse that you ride? Do people still ride them, or have they given way to automobiles and flying machines??

Enough for now. I must rest.

Your Friend in the Past,

Emma

Sam realized she hadn't answered Emma's question from the day before about personal airplanes. That would give her something to say. Something safe. When Sam had last written in the diary she was planning to tell Emma about her future. Now, that was really, really not a good idea. Maybe Emma would forget she had mentioned it.

June 25, 2014

You make me laugh.

What a lie. Sam was crying when she wrote it.

No, we don't have personal flying machines. Yes, there are

*a lot of airplanes and I have even ridden in them. But, no, I
don't own one. I do own a bicycle. That's what we rode to the
ice cave. I mostly ride a bike. It will be a few years before I can
drive.*

Sam so did not want to continue. Such a wuss. She was
bawling, now.

Got to go. Busy day ahead.

Your Future Friend,

Sam

Sam slid the diary back into its place on the shelf
and sat down at the computer. She dashed off an email to
Hailey.

Gaaaaaaawd!!!! I just sent Emma a message. It was awful
knowing when she's going to die. I can't even believe it.

Hailey wrote back so soon that it was almost like
texting.

Oh, you poor thing! I can't even imagine! It so sucks
On a second line, she wrote, I feeling kind of sucky. Going
back to bed for while.

***

Most of that day, Sam helped her mom around the
yard. She pulled weeds and fixed up some loose brick
edging that had gotten all cockeyed over the winter. It
wasn't hard work. Just boring, boring, boring. She listened
to music most of the time, which irritated her mother a
little, mostly because Sam did a lot of eye rolling whenever
her mom signaled for her to take out the earbuds so they
could talk.

When they went in for lunch, Sam checked her email.

Nothing from Hailey. She sent her one that read, *Feeling better, slacker?*

Early in the afternoon, before it got really hot, Sam's mom said they could knock off. She gave Sam $20 for the day's work. It was a little light, in Sam's opinion, but she didn't say anything. If she could earn enough to get close to the price of a phone, she hoped she could beg the rest of the way there. She could supplement a little with the money from the stamps, but she couldn't really use much of it. That would lead to questions she didn't want to answer.

Sam checked email. Nothing. She typed in, *Hello??? Are you still alive over there?* Then she thought better of it before hitting send. She erased it and typed, *How ya doin girl friend?*

When dinnertime came and went with no word from Hailey, Sam picked up the clunky handset of her folks' landline and dialed the Poulsens. She had keyed in the number from a list of written numbers her mom had posted next the phone. When it started to ring, Sam almost hung up. She'd really meant to call Hailey's cell. Mrs. Poulsen answered.

"Hello?"

"Uh, hi. This is Sam. Samantha. Is Hailey there?"

"Oh, deary, she's here, but she can't come to the phone. She's not feeling well at all. I'm a little worried about her."

"I'm sorry," Sam said. "Do you suppose she could talk on her cell?"

"Well, maybe. I'd rather she rested."

"Just for a minute. I promise."

"Well, all right, I guess. Just for a minute."

"Uh, Mrs. Poulsen? Do you have her cell number? I know it's stupid, but I don't know it. I usually text her and my phone is broke."

Mrs. Poulsen gave her the number. Sam hung up and punched it in. It went right to voice mail. She didn't bother leaving one.

JUNE 2014

Sunday	Monday	Tuesday	Wednesday	Thursday	Friday	Saturday
	2	3	4	5	6	7
8	9	10	11	12	13	14
15 B Day!	16	17	18	19	20	21
22	23	24	25	26	27	28 Duke Dies
29	30 She Dies					

June 26, 1914

I am so glad I make you laugh, Future Friend!

I think this will be short today. Not feeling any better. I am so peaked.

Your friend,

Emma

So, two friends feeling under the weather. Not much she could do about Emma, except write back and wish her well. For Hailey, she really had to go see her. She'd tried both email and Hailey's cell, again, without any response.

Sam showered and dressed. She bounced down the stairs to see if there was anything she could grab for breakfast. Maybe a banana?

As she looked in the fridge, the phone rang. Her mother picked it up in the living room. After a moment, her mom called, "Samantha, did I hear you come down?"

"Right here, Mom."

"Telephone," her mother said.

Sam grabbed the receiver from the wall phone in the kitchen.

"Hello, Hailey?"

"Uh, hello. No, this isn't Hailey."

Sam heard a click as her mother put down the extension.

"This is Jay... Mr. Baker. Actually, I'm looking for Hailey. I don't remember her last name," the science teacher said.

"Poulsen," said Sam. "But she's not answering her phone. She's been sick for a couple of days."

"Oh, I'm sorry to hear. That explains it, though."

"Explains what?"

"Well, she was going to drop by with the, uh, you know."

"The stamps."

"Those. I have her money for her."

"I'm sure she'll want it as soon as she feels better," Sam said.

"No doubt. I don't mean to be personal, but do you know what she has?"

"Not really. Flu or something, I suppose."

"Maybe just a summer cold," Baker said. "I feel like I'm coming down with something myself. Feeling just a little peaked today."

The man said it with two syllables, like peak-ed. It struck Sam as odd. She would say it as one syllable, like peakt. That's how she had pronounced it inside her head this morning when she read it in the diary.

"Well, thanks for letting me know," Mr. Baker said. Sam was only half-hearing him.

"Sure."

"Tell her to get better soon."

"Sure."

"Goodbye, now."

"Bye."

Sam stood there holding the receiver for a moment. Her mind had yet to put her thoughts into words. Nevertheless, her arms broke out in goose bumps.

***

Sam put her head down and pushed into the wind. Gravel and sand popped away from her tires as she pumped through. It was a coincidence. She kept repeating that inside her head as she went, the words sometimes forming on her lips. People got sick all the time. Knowing three people who were sick at the same time was not a miracle, especially when one of them was living a hundred years in the past. Four people, she realized. She did not know Emma's cousin Florence, but she knew she was sick. More, she knew she was soon to die. Crap, she *had* died, and so had Emma!

But, that was a hundred years ago, Sam thought. It was a c-o-i-n-c-i-d-e-n-c-e that Hailey was sick, too. Hailey had been sick before. Beaker had been sick before, too. Probably. Everyone gets sick. Still, she couldn't shake the feeling of dread that churned her stomach, which was banana free.

Sam skidded to a stop in front of the Poulsen house and dropped her bike on the lawn. Three of the boys played some kind of shooting game in front of the house, two with plastic guns and one with a long stick.

"She's sick, ya know," said Joel.

"Yeah, you canst go in," said Taylor.

"I know she's sick," Sam said. "I just need to see her."

Jacob said, "Aaron's sick, too. Mom told us to play outside so's we don't catch it."

"Aaron's sick?" Sam asked. "When did he get sick?"

"Just this morning," Jacob said.

Sam skipped the steps and jumped up on the landing to the house.

"Yous going to gets in trubber!"

"Stick it, Taylor," Sam said, under her breath. She knocked on the door.

She was about to knock, again, when Hannah opened the door a crack.

"Hi, can I come in?"

Hannah looked her up and down as if inspecting her clothes. She turned and yelled down the hall, "Mom, it's Samantha!"

Sam heard footsteps before the door opened a little wider, revealing Mrs. Poulsen.

"Oh, hello dear. Did you come to see Hailey?"

"Yes, I..."

"I'm not sure that's such a good idea," Mrs. Poulsen said. "She's got a fever. Aaron's got it, too. I wouldn't want you to catch it."

"I'll be careful," Sam said.

Mrs. Poulsen's lips squished up as she considered.

"Maybe you could stand in the doorway."

"I can't even go in her room?"

"Well, I don't know," Mrs. Poulsen said. "It's probably alright, but we don't know what she has, yet. I don't want anybody else getting sick."

"Okay, I promise. I won't go near her."

That seemed to satisfy the woman. Without another word she opened the door and motioned Sam inside.

The living room couch had a neat pile of sheets and blankets topped by a pillow stacked on the far end. Hannah, Sam thought. She's not sleeping in her own room, with Hailey. Sam passed down the hall through the miasma of hamsterness and paused in the doorway to Hailey's room. Her BFF was propped up with a couple of pillows at her back stacked against the wall. Hailey had a magazine in her lap. She stared at it, unfocused.

"Hi," Sam said.

Hailey looked up and gave her a weak smile.

"Hey, you."

"How are you doing?"

Hailey gave a one-shoulder shrug.

"Are you feeling any better?"

"Not really." Hailey sighed. "Just so weak."

"I got worried when you didn't answer your phone."

Hailey looked across her right shoulder to her nightstand.

"Probably dead," she said. "I haven't plugged it in for a

while. Can't reach it."

That was a strange thing to say. It was right there.

"Want me to plug it in?" Sam asked, and stepped into the room.

"No!" Hailey held up her left hand as if fending Sam off. "Don't get close. Might.." she dropped her arm. "Might catch it."

Sam felt as helpless as Hailey looked. She wanted to do something that could help her. Giving her access to her beloved phone seemed the best bet.

"What if I hold my breath? I can plug it in, then run out of the room."

Hailey shook her head. "I still couldn't reach it."

The skin above Sam's eyebrows bunched up.

"It's right there."

"I know, but I can't," Hailey said. "Just so weak. Can't hardly move my right arm at all."

Mrs. Poulsen came up behind Sam and said, "I think that's enough, dear. She really needs her rest."

"But..."

"I mean it Samantha. You really have to leave, now."

"Uh, bye, then," she waved at Hailey. "Get better soon. I'll be back."

Hailey nodded, then closed her eyes.

Mrs. Poulsen put her arm around Sam and walked her down the hall. Sam had a sudden urge to break away and run back into the room and... What? Charge Hailey's phone? Give her a hug? Tell her she was sorry? She kept walking, not listening to what Mrs. Poulsen was saying until they got to the door.

"And, I'll be sure to call you the minute I know anything else. Don't worry."

***

When Sam got home she raced to her computer and typed, Symptoms: weakness, paralysis on one side, fever. In a second, Google popped up several sites that described a disease called Bell's Palsy. She skimmed the text. Usually struck people from 10 to 40. More prevalent in people with diabetes and pregnant women. But the paralysis wasn't quite right. One side, yes, but facial muscles. People with Bell's Palsy slurred their words and drooled. That wasn't Hailey. At least, not yet.

It occurred to Sam how silly it was for her to try to figure out what it was that Hailey had, based on spending a minute with her from ten feet away. A doctor couldn't have done it. Yet, she and Hailey depended so much on what they learned from the internet, especially since the whole diary thing started. She couldn't have kept away from the keyboard.

She sat there in front of the computer, fingers poised. What else could she look up that might help? Then it came to her. Peaked.

Sam clattered the keys. The first definition was "having a peak, like a mountain." Definition two was more to the point. "Being pale, wan or emaciated." Sam didn't know what wan meant and didn't bother to look it up. The synonym listed said it all: Sickly.

Both Emma and Beaker had told her they didn't feel

well. Was it such a miracle they had both used that word to describe how they felt? Probably not. Still, it made her queasy. Maybe even a little peaked.

***

Sam called Mrs. Poulsen about 9 that night to check on Hailey. No change, Hailey's mother had said. Even so, Sam composed a long email to her friend expressing her hope for a quick recovery. When she moused over the send button Sam was struck by a horrible thought. What if Hailey never got to read it?

JUNE 2014

Sunday	Monday	Tuesday	Wednesday	Thursday	Friday	Saturday
1	2	3	4	5	6	7
8	9	10	11	12	13	14
15 B Day!	16	17	18	19	20	21
22	23	24	25	26	27	28 Duke Dies
29	30 She Dies					

Sam hadn't slept much. She kept going over everything in her mind, again and again. She even got up a couple of times in the middle of the night to do another symptom search. She didn't learn much.

When the clock read 8 am, Sam got up and pulled the diary off the shelf. Emma's short entry from the day before was the last thing on the page. It was her turn to write.

June 27, 2014

I hope you are feeling much better today. My friend, Hailey, is still really sick. At least, she was last night. I'm worried about her. I'm worried about you, too. Please write and tell me everything is okay.

Your friend,

Sam

That was kind of pathetic, Sam thought. She felt guilty for not writing more, but what would she say? The only thing on her mind was her sick friend. Friends, really.

Sam heard the phone ring, then the sound of her mother's voice. She could still hear muted conversation from below, even after the call had ended. Probably Rachel talking with her mother. Her dad would be gone to work by now. Unless it was a Saturday. Was it Saturday? No, Friday, she thought.

Footsteps padded up the stairs and toward her room. A soft knock, then Rachel saying, "Hey, you awake."

"Sure, c'mon in."

Rachel slipped through and backed the door closed. She leaned up against it as if she were trying to keep someone out.

"How are you?"

"Okay, I guess," Sam said. "What's up?"

"Probably nothing, really. But, you need to know about Hailey."

Rushing the words out, Sam asked, "What about her?"

"That was Mrs. Poulsen on the phone. Hailey had a hard time breathing last night, so they took her to the hospital."

"The hospital? Is she alright?"

"They've got her on a ventilator."

"That's like...?"

"To help her breathe," Rachel said.

"She can't breathe?" Sam felt tears come on. In her mind she pictured Hailey lying limp on a beach, people pressed around her and doing CPR. But, no, that was Rachel's friend, Katy.

"It's just to help her. To make sure she's okay."

"We've got to go!"

"No, we can't," Rachel said. "You can't. Mrs. Poulsen was really clear about that. She said they have her isolated."

"What's that mean?"

"They're keeping people away from her, that's all. They don't want anyone else getting sick." Rachel scowled. "Hey, are you feeling okay?"

No, in fact, she was not. She felt like a horse had kicked her in the chest.

"Sam?"

"I'm fine," Sam said. "Can you leave me alone, please?"

As soon as Rachel had closed the door Sam scrambled to put on a t-shirt and shorts. She tied on a pair of running shoes and was out the window in 30 seconds.

***

Fremont had maybe 7,000 people. The town was small, but it had its own hospital, because the nearest bigger town was nearly 50 miles away. Sam was born at the Fremont Hospital. In the fourteen years since, she had been back exactly twice: once to see the new Poulsen baby and once when her mother was visiting a sick friend. That time, she had waited in the car, so maybe it didn't even technically count.

Sam knew where the place was well enough. It was just a block off her normal route to school. She took that familiar route, then the one-block detour and dumped her bike on the sidewalk next to the emergency room entrance.

The big glass doors slid fast to get out of her way as she entered. There were a dozen chairs, several of them occupied by sick people and their relatives. One boy that Sam vaguely recognized as a high school kid sprawled in one of the chairs, practically prone. He had a makeshift bandage wrapped around one hand. It was a dirty brown.

Sam made a bee line for the reception desk.

"Hailey Poulsen," Sam said, a little out of breath.

The nurse held up her hand for a moment, finished what she was writing and looked up. "What can I do for you, Miss Poulsen?"

"No, I'm not... I'm looking for Hailey Poulsen. She's supposed to be in here."

"In the emergency room? I don't..."

"Well, the hospital. I don't know if she's right here. I'm looking for her is all."

"I came on at six. Don't remember a Poulsen. Girl your age?"

"Yes, my age."

"You a relative?"

The lie came so fast it stunned Sam. "I'm her sister."

The woman stroked a few keys.

"P-o-l-s-o-n?"

"No, with a U and an E. P-o-u-l-s-e-n."

"Okay. Here we go. Yes, she's been admitted. Came in last night. Looks like she's in ICU."

"What's that?"

"Intensive Care."

"Where's that?"

"It's right through... You know, I really should see some I.D. I don't think they'll let you in to see her, anyway, but I can direct you to the nurses station in ICU if you can show me a driver's license, or something."

"I don't drive," Sam said, through tight teeth.

"School I.D.?"

"Never mind," Sam said, and spun around to go. Which is when she saw the wheelchair. She hadn't noticed it when she came in. A middle-aged man was sitting in it talking to a nurse. Sam could see only the back of his head. A thought flashed into her mind. Beaker.

She mentally corrected that to show the respect someone in a wheelchair deserved. From the back, it looked like Mr. Baker, science teacher and lover of stamps.

***

Sam got nowhere in her effort to see Hailey. She went around to the main entrance to the hospital and through the front doors, giving the first person she saw the same spiel she had given the emergency room nurse. After a few minutes, someone showed her back to a waiting room. Waiting, in the room, were Mr. and Mrs. Poulsen.

Sam couldn't, at that moment, remember ever hearing Mr. Poulsen speak. Surely she must have heard him. Still, it startled her when he opened his mouth and said, "What's this?" His voice was very high for a man. Not squeaky, exactly, but better for a cartoon character than for someone's dad.

"How is she?" Sam asked Mrs. Poulsen.

"Oh, dearie, you shouldn't be here. They're not letting anyone see her right now, not even us."

"How is she?" Sam asked, more insistent this time.

"Not good," Mr. Poulsen said. That cartoon voice did not make her laugh.

"She was having such a hard time breathing last night," Mrs. Poulsen said. "They have her on a tube, now, so at least she's getting air."

"Why couldn't she breathe?"

"Well, we don't know that," said Mrs. Poulsen. "The doctors say it could be a lot of things. Maybe pneumonia, though they don't really think that's it. Her lungs aren't all that congested. She just can't seem to breathe well."

The questions and non-answers went on for a few more minutes. Sam gave up and slouched down into a chair, where she sat for the next three hours. When she heard the noon whistle go off in town—a holdover from factory days—she decided she should go home and check her diary.

***

June 27, 1914

Oh, Sam, I am sorry about your friend. I hope she gets better. I am no worse, though it is a good thing I am left-handed. I do not think I could hold a pen in my right hand. My arm is as limp as a noodle.

It makes me tired just to write. Must rest.

Best,

Emma

JUNE 2014

Sunday	Monday	Tuesday	Wednesday	Thursday	Friday	Saturday
1	2	3	4	5	6	7
8	9	10	11	12	13	14
15 B'Day!	16	17	18	19	20	21
22	23	24	25	26	27	28 Duke Dies
29	30 She Dies					

Sam had dozed off and on through the night. Most of it was spent trying to get comfortable and trying not to think about Hailey. The more she tried, the more she thought about her.

A little before 8, Sam gave up and dragged herself into the shower, hoping it might wake her up a little. She had her shirt, shorts and flip-flops on, her hair wrapped in a towel, when there was a knock on the door.

"Come in," she called.

"Hey," Rachel said, when she came through the door.

"Not you, again," Sam said.

Rachel's smile slid off her face.

"Sorry, I didn't mean you. I mean, I didn't mean that it was you I didn't want to see. I just didn't want..."

"It's bad, again," Rachel said.

"Hailey?"

"No better. That's not the bad part. Aaron's in the

hospital, too, and now Jacob has it."

When Rachel said Jacob, Sam could think only of the Jacob she and Hailey had seen in the old convertible that day on the road to the ice cave. She had seen him and his friends exactly once, and he was the Jacob that popped into her mind.

"Jacob? But, we didn't even get close."

"What?"

"We were, like, ten feet away..." Then it dawned on her. "Jacob? Hailey's brother, Jacob?"

"Yes, who did you think I meant?"

"Nobody," Sam said." She stared into the middle distance for a moment, processing this new information.

"You okay?"

"I'm... Did you say Aaron's in the hospital, too?"

"Yes."

"And Jacob, too?"

"Not yet, I don't think. He's sick though. Whatever it is must really be catching." Rachel frowned at her sister. "You sure you're okay?"

"Yeah, I guess."

Rachel put the back of her hand up against Sam's cheek to feel her temperature. The gesture got to Sam, simple as it was. She caught herself choking back a sob.

"You're a little warm,"

"Shower," Sam said. "I just got out."

"Yeah, that's probably it. We better take your temp just the same."

Sam nodded, and Rachel went down the hall and into

their parent's bedroom. Their mom kept the thermometer in the master bath.

When Rachel came back, Sam was still standing in the same spot.

"Tongue," Rach said.

Sam opened her mouth and lifted her tongue so her sister could slide the instrument beneath it. Sam hated the feeling of the thermometer under her tongue. It always seemed like she might gag on it, which was crazy. It was such a little thing and in no danger of sliding down her throat. After a minute Rach pulled it out and looked at the reading.

"Almost 100. That's a little high. We should tell Mom."

"No! Not yet. Really, I think it's just because of the shower. I feel fine."

"We really need to tell her, Sam. People are getting really, really sick."

Sam glanced over Rachel's shoulder to the bookshelf where the diary sat. Maybe there was another message. What if her mother wanted to take her to the hospital? What if she never saw the diary again?

"Give me an hour. We'll take it again, then. If it hasn't dropped we'll tell Mom, okay?"

Rachel considered for a moment, then said, "One hour?"

Sam nodded.

"Okay, but I'll be back. If it's not lower in an hour, I'm telling Mom."

Rachel turned to go, starting to pull the door of Sam's

bedroom closed. She stopped and said, "I'm leaving this open. No bugging out the window."

Sam rolled her eyes. "I won't. I know there's no point going to the hospital."

After Rachel left, Sam retrieved the diary and sat down in her computer chair to see if there was anything new. There wasn't. It was a new day, though, so that meant it was probably her turn to write, anyway.

June 28, 2014

Hi. I'm pretty bummed. Sad. You probably don't know what bummed means. Hailey is in the hospital. They have her on a ~~ventila~~ a machine that helps her breathe. Two of her brothers are sick. So is the guy we sold the stamps to. Whatever Hailey has, it's like she's passing it on to everybody. Not me. Not yet.

How are you?

I just remembered that today is the day that Duke gets killed. In your time, that is. I guess you already believe us, huh? It's not like you could get on a plane and fly to Sarajevo to prevent it from happening. I wonder how things would be different if you did.

Here, Sam signed the page and closed the diary. But her thoughts continued along the same lines. How could changing the past change the future? It was ridiculous to think Emma might have gotten to Europe, somehow, then prevented that guy from being killed. But, what if she had? Just, what if? Would that mean there wouldn't have been a World War I, or maybe even a World War II? Could it be that simple? Or, was the war going to happen no matter what?

So, the Duke was going to die—did die. So was Emma, on June 30, according to the genealogy website. Did. She did die. No matter how hard she tried, Sam could only think of Emma as being alive, right now.

Sam went to her computer and woke it up. She still had the tab for the family tree site open. She clicked on Emma's cousin, Florence. Today was her day to die. A bad day for Emma. And, Florence, of course. And the Duke.

Again, Sam clicked through the pictures under the Media Gallery tab. There was the one with the unidentified girl, the girl Sam was certain must be Emma. She looked at her for a long, long time.

Emma, if it was Emma, wore her hair in two buns, one on either side of her head, something like Princess Leia from Star Wars. Sam had always thought that looked goofy. Somehow, it looked sweet on Emma. She wore a dark dress—hard to tell what color it was from a black and white photo. The neckline scooped modestly in the front. Edging the scoop, then running along the shoulders and down the center of the long sleeves was an elaborate trail of lace, made up of rectangles with exes diagonally across them. The lace looped down from each rectangle to catch the corner of the next and the next. It was probably off white. It reminded Sam of a doily her mother had, the one she kept under the Waterford crystal bowl in the dining room. Someone in the family had made that a million years ago. Someone dead. Sam remembered her mother had called it ecru. For a long time she thought that was the kind of doily it was, or something, until her mom corrected her. It was the color, kind of a creamy yellow. Ecru lace, Sam thought.

There were other tabs on the site. One was for "facts and sources." Sam clicked on that and found links to census and cemetery records. Not much there. Another tab was labeled "comments." She clicked on that, next. Only one item. Someone had added a note that said simply, "She died of polio."

Sam gawked at those words. Could that be right? Did people really die from polio? Sam thought of wheelchairs and crutches when she thought of polio. She did a Google search and clicked on a medical site that came up.

The disease was really called poliomyelitis. Polio was just the shortened name. And, yes, right there in the first sentence, "sometimes causes death." There was an old photo of a girl in some kind of machine. The caption said it was an "iron lung," whatever that was. It looked like a big, chrome pipe, with all kinds of little doors and hatches bolted all over it. Only the girl's head stuck out from the top of the thing. She was smiling, which seemed just wrong to Sam. She scanned the caption until her eyes lit on the phrase "to assist in breathing."

And that was when her own breathing stopped, for a beat or two. She skimmed the rest of the material—there was a lot of it—and her eyes fell on the words "often the paralysis is asymmetrical." Helpfully, "asymmetrical" was hyperlinked to a definition, in case you didn't know what it meant. Sam knew, but she clicked it, anyway.

"On one side," she whispered. Patients often had

paralysis on one side. Some of them found it hard to breathe, so they were put in an iron lung. Or, nowadays, on a ventilator.

In the next two minutes Sam was dressed and out the window, exactly what she had told Rachel she would not do.

***

It was probably her imagination. She was pumping as hard as she could so, of course she'd feel a little weak. And out of breath. And a little feverish. She shook those thoughts from her mind and pressed on toward the hospital.

This time she knew where the front doors were, and where the waiting room was where she would find the Poulsens. She did find them, but that wasn't who she was looking for.

Mrs. Poulsen said, "Samantha!" when she burst through the door.

"Where's the doctor?" Sam asked, almost breathless.

"What?"

"The doctor. I need to talk with Hailey's doctor."

Mrs. Poulsen gave her a fish-mouth look.

"Now! I know what she's got!"

Mrs. Poulsen still couldn't seem to grasp what Hailey was saying, but quiet, dependable Mr. Poulsen did not hesitate. He took off down a gleaming hallway.

In a couple of minutes Mr. Poulsen came back, trailed by a man in light green hospital scrubs.

"Here she is," Mr. Poulsen said, pointing at Sam as if

he'd caught her stealing candy. Or, Sam thought, a lipstick.

"Are you Hailey's doctor?" Sam asked.

"One of them," he said.

"Then you've got to know what she has. She's got polio."

His forehead wrinkled when she said that.

"Polio?"

"Yes, can you cure that? You can, can't you?"

"It can't be polio. There hasn't been any in the United States in decades. There are a few cases in Africa, but it's nearly eradicated."

"It's polio," Sam insisted.

"Not in the U.S.," the doctor said. "Everyone is vaccinated for that."

Sam glared at Mrs. Poulsen. "Not everyone," Sam said. "You have to believe me. It's polio!"

"No, it can't... Oh, you've been looking up her symptoms, haven't you? On the Internet, right?"

Sam felt herself blush.

"No, I appreciate your concern, young lady, but I don't think we'll be diagnosing this off of Wikipedia."

Now she felt her cheeks really burn. How did he know it was Wikipedia she was looking at?

"But, it all fits," Sam said, not feeling as sure now, herself. "She can't move her arm on one side, she can't hardly breath. The fever..."

"Many diseases have similar symptoms. It's not polio. How would she have gotten polio?"

"Lipstick?"

"Lipstick?" The man hesitated. "Did she get lipstick from someone in Africa?"

"No, not Africa. Here. But, from a long time ago. When they had polio."

"What are you talking about?" Mrs. Poulsen asked. "Did that girl get more lipstick?"

Sam nodded.

The doctor said, "But not from Africa?"

"Not from Africa. But it was really, really old lipstick, from back when there was polio here."

The doctor gave a dismissive wave. "Wouldn't matter. The virus wouldn't live more than a day or so on lipstick."

"But, what if it..."

The man in the scrubs had already turned around and was striding down the hall.

She called after him, "What if it was frozen?"

He waved one hand behind him without looking back.

Sam could see it clearly, then. She saw herself telling the story of the diary, the story about the broken bottle, the ice cave and the bottle with the stamps. After that, she'd get around to telling about the lipstick. She'd do this to a succession of adults, none of whom were the least bit inclined to believe her. She would tell it again, and again, finally producing the diary itself, and maybe the video of the ghost writing. Still, no one would believe her. Oh, maybe someone would start to believe. It took she and Hailey some time to believe, after all. In the meantime, Hailey would get sicker and sicker. So would her brothers. So would Mr. Baker. If that was really Mr. Baker she had seen. So, even, might she.

Sam didn't have time for that.

She left the hospital waiting room as quick as she had entered, ignoring the questioning from Mrs. Poulsen behind her. Sam retrieved her bicycle from the grass in front of the building and started pedaling toward home. Her imagination exaggerated the weakness that was probably not there at all. She felt like her fever was spiking. Again, her racing mind. And, was she weaker? Not weak all over, but a little weaker on her left side? She pumped harder on that side to prove it wasn't so. She'd had her shots. That included polio, didn't it? And Beaker was a science teacher. He wouldn't skip vaccinations, would he?

Maybe it wasn't polio. Maybe there was some other awful disease Emma had sent into the future on a lipstick, something no one had been given a vaccination against. Maybe, if she spent more time on the internet she could find out what it was. Or, maybe it didn't matter what it was.

When she got home she raced through the house and up the stairs, where Rachel was just coming out her room, thermometer in one hand.

"Where have you been?" Rach asked.

"Riding. Scuse me," she said as she pushed past her big sister.

"Hey, it's time to take your temp."

"In a minute," Sam said.

"You promised you..."

Sam glared at her. "In. A. Minute!" She slammed the door, practically in Rachel's face. She didn't lock it, but

Rach didn't try the knob. Sam's insistence must have sunk in.

Sam pulled the diary down and began to scribble.

Same day. Emma, you've got to listen to me and do <u>exactly</u> what I say. This isn't going to make any sense to you, but if you believe I exist you have to do it. Cause, if you don't I might not exist any longer. Emma, Hailey might die! I might die! Only you can save us. PLEASE BELIEVE ME!!!!

I know you're sick, but you have to do this the instant you find this message. Tear out every page in this diary, then burn them! Make sure there is nothing left but ash. Then, put that in the trash, or bury it under a rock, or throw what's left of it in the river. GET RID OF IT SO NO ONE CAN EVER FIND IT!!! This is the most important thing you've ever done. PLEASE BELIEVE ME!

It wasn't until she had written all that that she saw just above it, these words.

June 28, 1914

I got the worst news today. My

And the entry ended there. Emma must have been writing it even as Sam picked up the diary. She had probably watched, fascinated, still a little afraid, as Sam scrawled her latest entry.

So, Sam added one more line.

So sorry about your cousin.

JUNE 2014

Sunday	Monday	Tuesday	Wednesday	Thursday	Friday	Saturday
1	2	3	4	5	6	7
8	9	10	11	12	13	14
15 B Day	16	17	18	19	20	21
22	23	24	25	26	27	28
29	30					

It was Sunday afternoon, so her dad had the day off, which meant he was working at the Big House. It was what her dad did nearly every weekend. Sam couldn't figure out why you'd work all week, then work some more on the weekend when YOU TOTALLY DIDN'T HAVE TOO!

This weekend, he had some help. Sam had screwed up and dropped her phone in the toilet, so her dad had conned her into helping him at the old house as a way to pay for a new one. She'd be 47 by the time she'd saved enough money for a new iPhone, as she had made perfectly clear to her father. What choice did she have?

To her surprise, her BFF, Hailey, had volunteered to help her, if her dad paid them both. Hailey was going to give the money to Sam. Anyway, most of it. She'd probably keep ten bucks for makeup.

And, just as surprising, Hailey found the Big House interesting, especially the post office desk in one corner of

the living room. She'd gone through some of the old letters
and asked a bazillion questions.

Old crap bored Sam. She had to admit it was a little
interesting to read some of the old letters.

Now, they were working upstairs. She and Hailey
had swept up most of the room, knocked down some
cobwebs—which totally creeped Sam out—and were now
moving some of the furniture so they could sweep behind
it.

When they moved the dresser you could see that the
wallpaper behind it was not as faded as on the rest of the
wall. This was the only room that had any wallpaper at
all, which was a blessing. It was awful. The wallpaper was
cream colored with a light blue design. The pattern was
a complex series of scenes. One showed a teenage boy on
the back of a horse gesturing to a teenage girl who was in
a full-length dress. At the girl's feet a toddler played on the
ground. Another scene was of a boy hunting with a spear in
his hand, which seemed out of place—all the figures looked
like they might have lived in Europe a couple of centuries
earlier, from the clothes they wore. The boy was blowing
through a decorated cow horn, while two dogs chased an
extravagantly antlered deer. Scattered through the repeating
scenes were grazing cows and leafy trees.

"Who picked out the hideous wallpaper?" Hailey asked.

"Really," said Sam. She glanced along the bottom of the
wall behind the dresser and noticed something.

"This is weird," she said, kneeling down. There was a
little rectangle in the wallpaper. It was like someone had cut

out a piece of wall and ever-so-carefully slipped it back in place.

Hailey knelt down as Sam slipped a fingernail into the crack. She wiggled and one end of what turned out to be a board eased out of the hole. Sam picked up the board to look at it. The wallpaper covered the front of it and was wrapped around every side and partway around the back of the board.

Hailey said, "Reach in there and see what you can find."

"*You* reach in. There's probably mice and spiders."

"I wish we had a light," Hailey said. She lifted the wallpaper-covered board and fitted it into the hole.

"Wow. Perfect! All the pictures match up."

"You'd never see it under the dresser unless you were looking for it."

"Maybe not then," Hailey said.

Sam ran her fingers across the board and found a little finishing nail, with little more than the head sticking up. Gripping it between her fingers she pulled. The board came right out.

Hailey took the wallpaper covered board from her.

"This kid on the horse needs a mustache," she said.

Sam was now sitting on the floor. Even so, she got so light headed when Hailey said that, she nearly fainted.

"What's the matter?" Hailey asked.

"I don't know," Sam said. "It's the weirdest feeling. Like, what do you call it when it seems like you've done something before?"

"Deja... something."

"That's it, deja vu. It's like we've had this same conversation in this very same spot."

"Really?"

"Really. Well, not now, but a second ago. It was just... really weird."

The little space in the wall where the board had been was maybe six inches by eighteen inches. Sam saw a glint of sunlight reflecting off something inside the hole. She bent down to get a better look. There was a jar inside the wall. That wasn't all. Sam saw the faintest glimmer coming from a tangle of web. A spider had used the jar as part of its construction strategy. Not just any spider. Sam could see the shiny black thing hanging upside down from the strands of its web. Waiting. There was a moment when the automatic fear started constricting her throat; when her muscles tensed for a mad scramble away from the opening. But something made her stay, crouched there on the floor in front of this secret place. A fragment of conversation came back to her: "It's not like they can fly or anything." Had Hailey said that? When? In the seconds she took to think of that, the feeling of panic passed. Sam felt a calm come over her and a solid resolve start to build.

A part of her couldn't believe what she did next. A vanishing voice screamed inside her head to run, run! She reached into the openning and put her fingers around the jar, pulling it out of the opening, ripping it from the rigging of the web. The spider was the one that scrambled. In a panic it pulled itself up through its failing web and out of sight into the wall.

"What's that?" Hailey asked.

"Just an old bottle," Sam said. "A ball jar."

"A what jar?"

Sam ignored her and turned the bottle so she could read through the glass the two words written on a scrap of paper inside: "I believe."

Made in the USA
Charleston, SC
18 November 2015